Death by Misadventure

Death by Misadventure

ESTELLE THOMPSON

St. Martin's Press
New York

20779

Thompson, Estelle.
    Death by misadventure / Estelle Thompson.
        p.   cm.
    "A Thomas Dunne book."
    ISBN 0-312-06947-2
    I. Title.
PR9619.3.T447D4   1992
823—dc20   91-41107
                                                                      CIP

First published in Great Britain by Robert Hale Limited under the title *The
Substitute*.

First U.S. Edition: April 1992
10 9 8 7 6 5 4 3 2 1

Death by Misadventure

One

I was six years old and sitting on my father's knee when the police came and took him away.

I didn't know then that they were police, of course. They were just two men in business suits and my father went with them almost as if he had been expecting them, and I didn't think anything much of it. Only he never came back and I never saw him again.

My mother became pale and silent. I remember that, because she stayed that way, in a sense, until she married George Marsh when I was eleven, and even then the scars of my father's sudden exit from our lives never really left her.

She never talked to me about my father, even at first, when I would keep asking when he was coming back, never believing her terse: 'He isn't coming back. Not ever.'

It was at school I learned why. The other children took delight in taunting me, of course. Even now I remember with photographic clarity one little blonde, blue-eyed girl who looked like an angel chanting, 'Your father's a murderer; your father's a thief!'

That was the first time I heard it, and I remember flying at her, screaming, 'He is not! He is not!' And hitting her, and a teacher pulling us apart.

Even then I think I knew, with a terrible sickness in my stomach, that the blonde child wasn't making the story up.

After maybe a year – when, I suppose, the trial was long over – we moved to another town, and by then my father's crime was just another statistic and people had forgotten, and left us alone.

But the memory never left me alone. It hung always in the back of my mind, like the ache of an old scar that would wake to dull throbbing at unexpected moments. In my early teenage years I cherished vague romantic dreams of investigating the crime for which my father had been sentenced to life imprisonment, and proving him innocent by some brilliant stroke of deduction.

That dream had faded when in later years I checked old newspaper files and then secured the transcript of the trial. That made it patently clear that Roger Sutton was a thief at least, because he had pleaded guilty to breaking and entering a jewellery store with intent to steal. He had used his knowledge as a plumber who had earlier done repairs on the building, and gained entry through the roof without triggering any alarms. But he claimed that someone had beaten him to it, and he stuck to that highly unlikely story: the safe and the showcases were empty of anything worth stealing, except for one pendant; and the patrolling security officer was already dead in the lane at the back of the store.

The police said, when there was no trace of the missing jewellery, that either Roger had hidden it or he had an accomplice. Roger denied both. None of his story convinced the police, which was hardly surprising, and it didn't convince the jury, either.

It didn't convince me, in my turn. Two attempts to rob the same store on the same night? Credibility could be pushed only just so far.

But it did leave me with the faintest of hopes that there was somewhere some mitigating circumstance or a loose end that wouldn't tie with anything else. I had known for a long time that I had to find my father. Before I could know who I was, what sort of blood, what sort of genes I carried, I had to see my father for myself, had to make my own judgment, not that of a jury presented only with a given amount of evidence.

I had to have him tell me what had happened that night.

And, as my mother had pointed out when she learned of my plans, how would I know whether what he told me was the truth, even then?

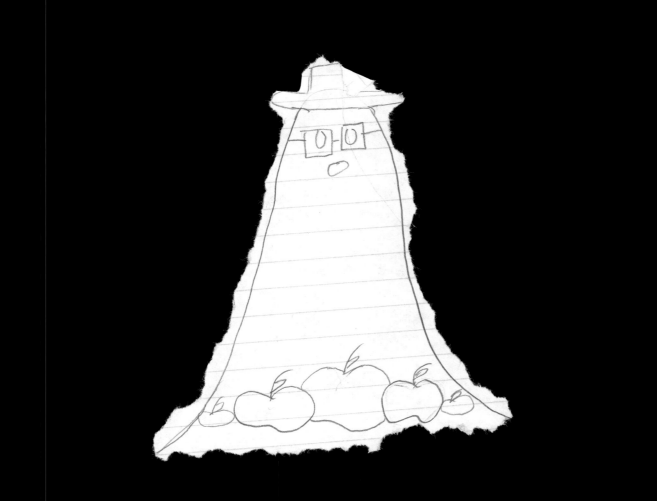

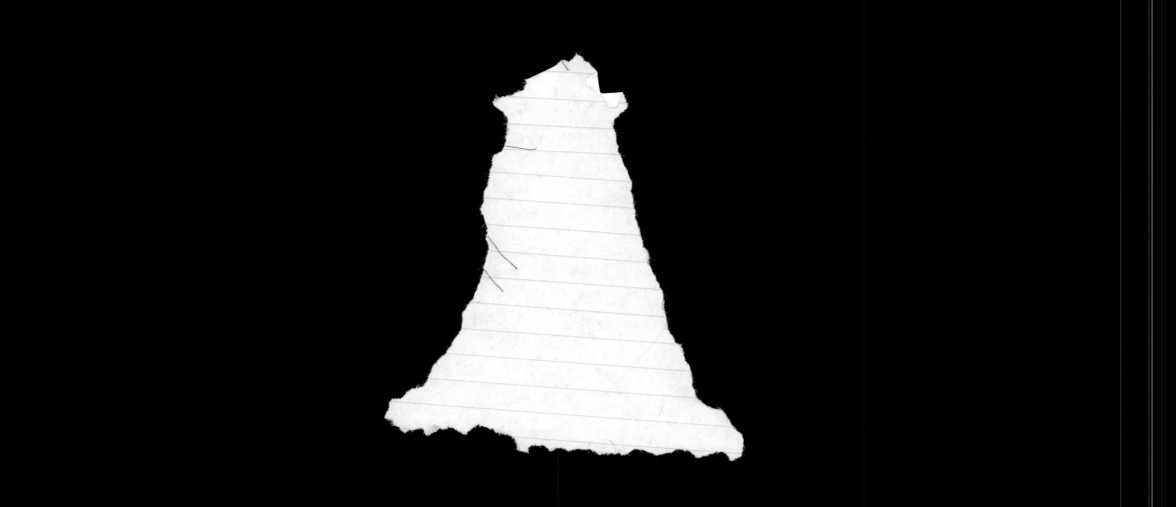

Now my search had brought me here from my central Queensland home to southern New South Wales and a small town I'd never seen.

I stopped the car on the outskirts of town. There was a row of cottonwood poplars just coming into their bright autumn dress and I got out of the car and walked on to the wooden bridge they framed and stood for a while looking down at the stream below, perhaps hoping that something of the tranquil beauty would ease the knot of anxiety in my stomach.

Roger Sutton had been released from prison seven years ago, after serving twelve years of his sentence. From then, to all intents and purposes, he had dropped out of the bottom of the world. When any lines of enquiry I could think of all ran off into nothing, I had hired a private investigator and he, costing more than my secretarial job could afford, had been good.

He had found – fortunately before his fees sent me bankrupt – that Roger Sutton had changed his name to Roger Miller, married a widow with two teenage children, and established his own plumbing business here in this town.

At least, all my private eye would say was that this was correct according to his information. He hadn't offered to make a refund if his information proved incorrect.

So I had given up my job and told my friends I was going to take a long vacation to spend some time on my hobby of landscape painting – which, I cherished a very secret and faint hope, might one day become more than a hobby. I had come armed only with an old snapshot of my father which his sister had given me – my mother having carefully destroyed every trace of Roger Sutton in our household. If Roger Miller bore no resemblance to the lean, black-haired young man whose dark eyes smiled at me in the photograph, then I would know the private investigator's information was wrong, and I had wasted my time.

And if, when I saw him, there was a chance Roger Miller was the man in the photograph, I had no idea what I was going to say. I had rehearsed a dozen opening remarks or questions. All now seemed incredibly stupid. Perhaps when I saw him I would know what to say.

A little gust of wind sent a shower of leaves from the cottonwoods tumbling around me like a flurry of white-and-gold snowflakes and I walked back to my car. I stopped first at a real-estate agent's office and asked if he had a flat or small house to let for two or three months.

The agent, a short stocky man with blue eyes alert with many years of assessing people and what they could afford, smiled and briskly shuffled some papers. 'Yes, I think I might have the very thing. Charming little place called Amber Cottage, large garden, even a tennis court. The owner has gone overseas for six months and put the house up for rent. It's almost right out of town, but if you have a car you probably wouldn't mind.'

I didn't mind in the least, especially when I saw the cottage – small, delightfully designed and set in a large rambling garden where liquidambers, from which it clearly took its name, blazed in their autumn glory of gold and amber and deep red.

It was fully furnished, the rent was reasonable and I said at once it would suit me very well. 'There is one condition,' the agent said after the formalities of checking my credentials, putting up a bond against damage, and such things. 'The owner insists that whoever occupies the place must look after the garden. That's a written condition.'

I assured him I would enjoy taking care of the garden and, having dealt with the legalities, shopped for food and unpacked my suitcase, I stood for a minute in the little living-room where a couple of easy chairs were drawn up in front of a log fire waiting to be lit.

This was the moment I had worked to achieve for so long – provided the private investigator was right – and suddenly I found my stomach muscles had knotted and my hands were sweating. The long hunt was over, and I didn't know how to handle my quarry.

Perhaps, I thought, I should leave it till tomorrow to confront Roger Miller. It was late in the day now; he might even have stopped work and gone home. 'You're a coward, Lyndal Sutton,' I said firmly, aloud. 'This is what you came for. Get on with it before you find some excuse to pack your bags and head home. And if you can't face the reality of what your father is, you'll never face reality at all.'

I snatched my purse, almost ran out to the car before I could change my mind, and drove slowly through the town in search of a plumber. I found the place in a side street, the shop-front lettering saving me any enquiries by declaring: Millers' Plumbing and Draining. A neat shop with plumbing supplies of all kinds displayed, and what was obviously a workshop behind it. Not fancy. Not down-at-heel. Roger Miller had a solid small business, it appeared.

A youngish woman in a half-walled office came to the counter and asked pleasantly if she could help me. My father's wife? I wondered.

'I'd like to see Mr Miller if that's possible,' I said, wondering if my voice betrayed how dry my mouth had become.

'I'll see if he's come in — he was out on a job,' the woman said, and called through the door of the workshop, 'George, is Mr Miller back yet? There's a lady to see him.'

'He's just unloading some gear in the yard,' a young man in overalls said, coming to the door and glancing at me. 'I'll see if he can come. It's nearly knock-off time,' he added, not unpleasantly.

'That's all right,' I said quickly. 'It's just a small thing — not a job I want him to do. I'll go through to the yard, if I may.'

'Sure,' George said cheerfully. 'Through that door there. Don't trip over that piping, mind.'

'Thanks,' I said.

It's just a small thing: I only want to know if he's my father.

He was dressed in blue overalls, standing with his back to me, doing something with pipes on the back of a small truck. He had black curling hair cut short and flecked with grey, and he was tallish and lean and moved with a precision which said he was whippy-tough and muscular, and the thought ran through my mind that he could be a nasty opponent in a fight.

'Mr Sutton,' I said. It was a statement, not a question.

His body stiffened with a slight jerk that gave him away, and perhaps he knew it. It might have been a long time since he had heard that name, but he had reacted instinctively.

He turned, carefully casual, but his dark eyes were not smiling as they did in my photograph and in my memory, and a neatly-trimmed beard, grey-flecked like his hair, so totally changed his appearance that I could never have been sure, except for that betraying reflex response to hearing his name.

'Sorry,' he said. 'You must be in the wrong place. There's no one of that name here.'

'I think there is,' I answered quietly, trying to keep my voice steady.

His eyes narrowed. 'Look, lady, my name's Miller, my apprentice's name is Walsh, the lady in the office is Mrs Hill. That's the entire staff.'

'Your name may be Miller now, but it wasn't always, was it?' Again, it was not really a question.

He made a sharply impatient gesture. 'I'm sorry, I don't know what you're talking about.' Then – quickly, incisively – 'Who the hell are you?'

'I'm Lyndall Sutton. I'm your daughter.'

Whatever shock he may have felt, his face was totally blank and nothing but the strung-out silence gave the slightest hint of any emotion whatever.

Then he shrugged and shook his head. 'You're one of those adoption cases moving mountains of red tape to find your real parents, are you? Sorry, miss. I'm afraid your information's been wrong. My name is Miller and I have no daughter. Now, if you'll excuse me, I have to unload the rest of this gear. That lane way will take you back out to the street.' He lifted a tool-box out of the truck and took it into the workshop, shutting the door behind him.

I walked through the lane to my car and drove back to

the cottage, my thoughts in a tangle. Whatever I had expected, whatever possible scenarios I had rehearsed in my mind, I hadn't ever considered such total dismissal, even though probably I should have. He had been very convincing. But for that split-second involuntary reaction to hearing the name he was born to, I would almost have been prepared to believe him.

The last rays of the day's sun back-lit the colours of the trees at the cottage to glowing splendour as I drove up, and the large kitchen which served also as a dining-room was filled with sunlight as if nature was trying to warm and soothe the cold excitement that was clamping hard fingers just below my ribcage. I made coffee and sat at the pine table sipping it and wondering whether people usually felt this bewildering tumult of emotions when confronted with a long-lost parent – especially one who didn't want to know them.

It must happen all the time, of course, to people who had been adopted in infancy and later felt compelled to find their natural parents, whatever the circumstances. My father had been very quick to come up with that pretended assumption that I was one of them. Had he long been half-prepared for me to try to find him? If so, he had been equally long prepared to reject me?

I didn't know how long I'd been sitting there at the table, but then a knock at the door roused me from my thoughts, the sun had set, the dusk had filled the kitchen and my coffee was stone cold. The rap at the door came again, impatiently, and I jumped up and fumbled for the unfamiliar light-switch, calling, 'Coming!' for fear he might go away. I had no doubt that my father had had a change of heart and had sought me out. I wondered fleetingly how he had known where to find me.

A tallish young man with wavy blond hair, wearing a leather jacket and holding a motorcyclist's helmet, handed me a letter.

'Sorry to disturb you,' he said, 'but I was asked to deliver this.' Dark blue eyes swept me and the cottage with a second's frank curiosity, then he nodded and strode off down the path as I mumbled thanks.

Not a visit from my father. But very likely a note from him. It wasn't addressed, I noted, as I turned it over and tore open the envelope, fumbling with anxious haste.

It was a typewritten note which began: *Dear Lillian.*

I moved quickly back to the door to call to the motorcyclist that the note was not for me, but as I opened the door I heard the bike start up and roar off back into town.

Surely Roger wouldn't have gone to the length of pretending he had forgotten my name? I glanced at the note again, not wishing to read a letter that wasn't mine, but needing to be sure it wasn't meant for me. By the time I had read the first two lines I knew I was going to read it all, even though clearly it was not mine. On a single sheet of paper, it was a desperate plea:

> *Please help me. There is no one else I can ask. I am going to be killed. You must not go to the police. Ivan would laugh and make a joke of it and of course they would believe* him, *not me. But once they began asking questions it would be plain that I know what is to happen, and it would only happen sooner. It will look like an accident, but it will be murder. I know you and I had a quarrel but this is more important. Please, please believe me and do exactly as I ask. Come on Wednesday at 2 p.m. Don't say anything to anyone — not even to me, not even if we are alone. That is very important. Very, very important. I will explain in time. Wait for me to talk about it. Please. I am so afraid.*
>
> *Vi.*

All typed, and having the appearance of having been typed in frantic haste.

And underneath, as a postscript, two words: *Drive slowly.*

I stood stunned and disbelieving. Dear God, what had I blundered into? Or, more accurately, what had blundered into me?

Two

I went back to the kitchen and sat at the table to read the note over and over, almost as if by doing so I could make it read differently.

Not my note. But dare I say it was not my responsibility? A woman in terror for her life had begged for help.

Lillian. It was Lillian who had been asked to help, not me. Presumably Lillian was the owner of Amber Cottage and the estate agent had said she was away for six months. Maybe I could phone her. Then she was the one who'd have to make the decisions.

I found the agent's after-hours number and dialled it. Trying to sound cheerfully casual, I apologized for calling him at home. 'I wondered if you could tell me the name of the owner of the cottage and where I might contact her? There's a locked pantry cupboard and I can't find the key – of course she may not want the cupboard used, and if so that's quite all right, but it would be handy for me to use. And maybe the key's just here in some place that's so obvious I can't see it.'

I was babbling, I thought exasperatedly; if I didn't stop he'd realize there was something wrong.

He sounded as if he was used to such trivia. 'I'm sorry, Miss Sutton, but Miss Ballard's gone overseas – Trans-Siberian Railway and later some walking in Norway or somewhere, I believe – Lillian's an adventurous soul. Then she intends visiting various European countries, but no fixed itinerary.'

I forced a little laugh. 'A shade hard to catch up with her to ask about a key, then.'

'If I could be of any help –?' With the faintest of inferences that he hoped he couldn't.

'Oh no, it's quite all right,' I assured him. 'It doesn't matter at all. Thank you very much.'

I put the phone down. It did matter. It mattered a great deal. Lillian's an adventurous soul. Bully for Lillian. This was an adventure she was welcome to, and certainly not something I wanted thrown in with the use of the tennis court.

That note was none of my business, I tried to tell myself. The writer was probably eccentric, the victim of some kind of persecution mania – probably wrote notes like that all the time, and all her friends and family knew to ignore them.

But I didn't know, and Lillian wasn't around to ask, and so the ball was in my court. A woman had begged for help, and that cry might well be genuine. I desperately wanted to take the letter to the police – which Vi, whoever she was, implored Lillian not to do, and she had advanced a logical-sounding argument against seeking police help. The alternative was that I should try to deal with it myself, to take over whatever role it was that Lillian might have played. It was a prospect I found mountainously alarming.

Since there was no clue to Vi's identity, the first thing I should do was to find the man with the motorcycle who had delivered the note. In a town of this size there was a reasonable chance he knew the woman who had given it to him. I put on a jacket against the evening chill and drove slowly into town, acutely aware that my chances of finding the motorcyclist were fairly remote.

He had probably dropped in the note on his way home from work, but I calculated there was just a chance he would stop for a drink before he went home. On the basis of our few seconds' acquaintance I was surprisingly sure I would know him again, and in spite of my ignorance of motorcycles I had noticed his was a rather new-looking red-and-white machine – though there were probably two dozen identical ones around town, for all I knew.

There was a similar machine parked outside the second

hotel I checked, and I found the fair-haired bikie eating a counter tea alone in the smoky lounge bar. He glanced up and saw me as I walked towards his table, and at once got to his feet with what seemed to me singularly un-bikie-like courtesy, though even then I realized that there were bikies and bikies. He indicated a chair across the table and said, 'Is it fate, or were you looking for me?'

'Looking for you. I wanted to ask you about the lady who gave you the note to deliver to me. Is she someone you know?'

He hesitated as if reluctant to talk about it. 'No,' he said. 'No one I know.'

'What did she look like? I mean – I know this sounds idiotic, but the writing was so bad – a bit like my own – I couldn't make out the signature, and the note was an invitation. I'm going to seem awfully rude if I ignore it, and I honestly can't decipher who sent it.'

He looked at me intently, a strangely appraising look, then shrugged. 'It was no one I knew and I didn't take any particular notice. I was just handed the note and ten dollars and asked to take the letter right away to the lady in Amber Cottage. Someone gives me ten bucks to take a two-minute ride, I don't knock it back.'

'I see,' I said, standing up. 'Thanks anyway.'

As I walked to the door I had a strange feeling that he watched me every step of the way.

That night I sat for a long time in front of the log fire in the living-room, feeling exhausted by the day's events while at the same time my brain was intensely active, though my thoughts always came back to their starting-point with nothing achieved. I had only two facts to work on: I had found my father and he refused to know me, and a woman – somewhere, someone, sane or not – had begged for help to save her life.

The first problem, I had time to work on; I could perhaps learn something of Roger Miller even if he would never admit to being Roger Sutton. But as for the second, I might have only a few hours. The note had said: *Come on Wednesday at 2 p.m.* That was tomorrow, and by the time I finally went to bed the appointed time was only twelve hours away.

Over and over two sentences from that letter went through my beleaguered brain: *Please help me. There is no one else I can ask.* Why was there no one else to ask for help but someone with whom Vi had already quarrelled? Didn't she know anyone else? Didn't she trust anyone else? Had all her other friends and acquaintances already tired of receiving pleas from an unbalanced mind?

And above everything, what in Heaven's name was Lillian expected to *do*?

I was waiting outside the estate agent's office when he arrived for work and he quickly managed a smile to cover the fleeting oh-no-not-that-woman-again look of recognition.

'Hello, still having trouble with that cupboard door?'

'No, I feel foolish over that – it wasn't locked at all, just temporarily stuck. So silly of me to bother you over such a trifling thing. I do apologize. But now I'm afraid I've come to make a nuisance of myself again.'

'Not at all.' He was unlocking the office door. 'Come in and take a seat. How can I help you?'

As the note had mentioned Ivan it seemed probable that Ivan was Vi's husband, so I had decided to gamble on that.

'I imagine in your business you get to know a lot of people,' I said. 'I know this is a long shot, but do you happen to know a couple whose first names are Ivan and Vi? I met them on a cruise once and they were most insistent that if I ever found myself in this area I should look them up. I would very much like to, but unfortunately I've totally forgotten their surname – I'm dreadful at names and I guess I didn't really think it was likely I'd ever be here. I know I'm being a fearful pest, but I wondered if by any chance the names ring a bell with you.'

He smiled cheerfully. 'Yes, that sounds like the Norrises – a couple in their forties – oh, he'd be more than that, fifty plus, I would think. Might they be the ones?'

'Yes, indeed,' I said eagerly. The chances of there being

two couples named Ivan and Vi were remote. 'Norris. Do you know where they live?'

'Yes, I do, though I didn't actually sell them their house when they moved here a few years ago. I'll write down directions on how to get there – not that it's very complicated, but it's a few kilometres out of town and you take an unsealed road up a mountain. It's a perfectly good road, though, and they have a large, charming old house with great views down the river valley. You mentioned yesterday you wanted to do some landscape painting, so I should think you'd find good subjects out there, and I'm sure they wouldn't mind, even if they turn out not to be the people you're looking for.'

He was obligingly scribbling down directions on right and left turns as he talked. 'They seem nice people, though I can't say I know them well. Keep pretty much to themselves, especially since the boy's accident.'

'Oh?' I said questioningly, anxious to urge as much information from him as I could.

'Mmm. Not their son – adopted or something, I understand, but you probably know about that – boy about twelve or fourteen. Accident put him in a wheelchair quite some months back, poor kid.'

'That's very sad.' I meant it, but my mind was not really on the child's misfortune, except to think it might be possible that distress over her adopted son's disaster may have brought on some kind of emotional collapse for Vi, triggering frightening fantasies.

I would certainly prefer to think that desperate note was the product of a disturbed imagination, not the plea of a clear and reasoning mind. I decided to chance a remark that was in fact a probing question. 'I fancy Vi herself had some kind of health problem – nerves or something like that.'

The agent shrugged cheerfully. 'Could be. Can't say I heard anything about it, but I don't really know them personally.'

I thanked him warmly for his help and hoped nothing in my manner betrayed how apprehensive I felt. I was getting into something I had no idea how to handle, and if Vi Norris was right her life might depend on me, and she didn't know it.

What had she expected Lillian Ballard to do? Over and over that question hounded me. Whatever it was, she couldn't expect her husband to do it. *Ivan would laugh and make a joke of it, and of course they would believe* him, *not me.* Why would Ivan laugh and make a joke of it? Because the idea was unbelievable? Or because it was Ivan himself she was afraid of? And why would the police automatically believe Ivan's scepticism and not Vi's fears? The answer to that seemed most likely that Vi had a previous record of groundless fears, suggesting some kind of nervous breakdown in the past. Or could it be that a threat to her life was so improbable no one was going to believe her story, and whatever had happened to trigger her fears was something for which she could produce no evidence?

Did she think Lillian could find the evidence to convince others there really was a threat? Maybe she wanted Lillian to stay with her as some sort of security against an attempt – or another attempt – on her life, a security Ivan didn't provide.

It kept coming back to Ivan, however many times I turned the possibilities over in my mind, but whether Ivan was failing her simply because he couldn't believe her, or because he was the threat, I couldn't know. And in any case, maybe the threat was only a dark nothingness lurking among the shadows of a disturbed mind. An ugly dream that for Vi did not melt in the warm light of day the way bad dreams are supposed to do.

Shadow or substance? It would probably take a psychiatrist a whole series of expensive consultations to find out, and I had to try it from the depths of ignorance. I felt like a female Don Quixote sallying forth to fight demons which would probably turn out to be non-existent.

I hoped so.

According to the estate agent's directions the Norris house was about ten kilometres out of town, so I tried to time my arrival for the requested time of 2 p.m. As I left town I drove past Miller's Plumbing and Draining but I saw no one about and I tried to shut Roger Sutton out of my mind for the moment. After this afternoon, with luck, that would be the only major problem on my agenda, but for the moment I had to concentrate on someone else's troubles.

The road ran quickly out of town and through a green valley where Poll Herefords grazed with easy purposefulness, here and there lifting a white head to glance with disinterest at my car; past a dairy farm or two with Friesians black and white as a chequer-board against the pasture. And everywhere poplars and willows and elms and other northern hemisphere imports clustered in splashes of brilliance against the quiet grey-green natives as summer went from the valley, trailing glory defiantly behind. There was an orchard or two, some trees still red-dotted with apples, and as the road began to climb there were sheep nibbling with endless intensity on the hillsides.

Wrens skittered through the grasses beside the road, and a magpie on a fencepost carolled liquid sound that spilled for a moment into my consciousness above the sound of the car's engine. Over it all lay the warming golden invisibility of sunlight.

And high above in the clear blue, a wedge-tailed eagle swung in slow searching circles – death on magnificent wings.

Peace was an illusion.

My directions turned me on to an unsealed road which wound up a timbered mountain. *Drive slowly*, the note had said. Why? Perhaps the road was rough, somewhere up ahead. I drove cautiously.

The road crossed a ridge and came out above another valley, with just tantalizing glimpses through the trees. Then as I rounded another bend there was a sapling down, virtually blocking the road. I had adequate time to stop, and probably would have, even if I hadn't been more or less expecting some kind of traffic hazard, and the sapling was small enough for me to drag aside without difficulty. Even if someone had driven headlong into it, it was doubtful if it would even have caused damage to the paintwork. Nevertheless I felt a small prickle of apprehension as I pulled the obstacle aside. Drive carefully. And now I was presented with a reason, but whether it was the sort of reason Vi had in mind, I had no idea.

You're being absurd, I told myself. What could possibly be the point of anyone putting a tree across the road – a tree I could easily pull aside? I looked at the roots of the sapling and at the embankment above. Clearly the sapling had toppled from there on to the road, and there was nothing to indicate it hadn't done so due entirely to natural causes. The whole thing was so totally harmless.

At least it was harmless to anyone in a car, I reflected as I heard a motorcycle start up somewhere. If someone on a bike had hit it, it might have been a bit nasty. But it seemed unlikely Lillian Ballard rode a motorcycle, and the thought of anyone wanting to set a trap for her or for anyone else was ridiculous. Such thoughts were, however, some indication of the state of my nerves.

I got back into the car and drove on. A couple of hundred metres further on rain had washed a rough gutter across the road and I smiled to myself: there was the reason for the caution to drive carefully. Abruptly I was out into a large clearing and I had arrived at the Norrises' house, a big Colonial-style house of sandstone-coloured brick with wide verandahs, a sweep of lawn and clusters of shrubs and trees. To the north it looked down on a narrower valley than the one I had just driven through, and, fairly distantly to the south-east there was a sheet of sky-reflecting blue water – part of one of the dams of the Snowy Mountains hydro-electric scheme, I presumed. A couple of hundred metres from the house, like a miniature of its distant cousin, a small household-supply dam with a cluster of reeds at one end was rippled by busy water-fowl.

I got out of the car and stood for a few moments looking at the scene with artist's eyes and absorbing its beauty. Then I was reminded of the eagle hunting in the next valley, and I wondered with a little shiver whether death hung over this lovely place also.

A woman sat reading in a little sheltered courtyard beside the house, and she put her book aside and stood up at my approach. Any surprise or disappointment she may have felt at seeing a total stranger didn't show by the time I was close enough to have seen it. A suntanned woman in early-to-middle forties, slender and wiry-looking, with dark hair cut short in a style which suited her, she watched my approach with an unsmiling intensity which was neither hostile nor welcoming, but seemed somehow rather more than the normal neutrality with which anyone might meet an unexpected stranger on an unknown mission.

If I had been selling encyclopaedias I couldn't have put on a better-prepared smile. 'Mrs Norris?'

Green eyes assessed me. 'Yes.'

'My name's Lyn Sutton. I'm a sort of amateur artist looking for areas that appeal to me – I do landscapes. Please forgive me for intruding, but your home and its views were suggested to me as something I might like to paint, and I wondered if you and your husband would mind awfully if I did some sketching some time? I promise I wouldn't be any kind of a nuisance, but I know it's pretty cheeky of me to ask.'

Vi Norris hesitated for a second and then smiled. 'I don't see any reason why you shouldn't do any painting or sketching you like,' she said pleasantly. 'I'm sure my husband wouldn't mind either.'

'Wouldn't mind what?' a big fair-haired man asked cheerfully as he came along the verandah. 'Hello,' he added, nodding to me.

'This young lady does some landscape painting,' Vi told him. 'She'd like to do some sketches here. This is my husband, Ivan,' she added to me. 'Miss – Hutton, was it?'

'Sutton,' I said. 'Lyn Sutton. Not everyone likes having someone hanging about, doing sketches of their houses or even any part of their property. But I would be most grateful for the opportunity to try capturing something of

this.' I waved my hand encompassingly. 'If I wouldn't be
an intrusion.'

He hesitated, and then laughed lightly. 'I hardly think
you'd do the place any harm by painting pictures of it. Of
course you may. You're most welcome.'

He sounded as if he meant it, but I had the feeling that
for a moment he had regarded the prospect as disturbing.
But no doubt that was coloured by my imagination, and it
was perfectly true that sometimes people had flatly refused
to allow me to paint so much as a tree on their property,
seeing it as an intrusion on their privacy, and it was a
view-point I had always been ready to respect. I was glad I
hadn't encountered it here.

The Norrises could scarcely have been more pleasantly
co-operative. While she was much less talkative than Ivan,
it was Vi who suggested I might like to see the aspect down
the valley from the verandah because it provided the
foreground of the garden. 'I've no idea whether you'd feel
that enhanced it or not,' she said, 'but it's better to see
things from all angles, I should think.' There was nothing
in her attitude which suggested she was expecting a visit
from anyone else, but there was a kind of watchfulness
about her which could have indicated either nervous
tension or simply an intensity of character which some
people exude and which I have always found faintly
disconcerting – a feeling that they are always profoundly
concentrated on whatever they may be doing, from
discussing philosophy to peeling an apple.

Presently, though, she suggested that Ivan might show
me through the garden and up the path to the 'Fairy
Wood', where I might like the angle of the house. I
wondered whether, while we were gone, the phone was
ringing in Amber Cottage, with no Lillian to answer it;
which made me wonder, as I had done before, why the
plea for help hadn't been made by phone in the first place.

'Fairy Wood?' I asked as Ivan and I walked.

He smiled. 'Peter's name for it – our foster-son. There
are lots of fairy wrens there, and they're favourites of his,
though he likes all the birds. Of course, there aren't as

many varieties there in winter, as many migrate. Do you live somewhere near?'

'No, I'm a Queenslander, so naturally I'm in love with the autumn colours, because in the more tropical areas we don't get them, of course. I'll have to be careful I don't overdo them and just turn out picture postcards.'

'Are your paintings good?' Somehow he asked the blunt question without making it in the least offensive.

'Perhaps they might be, one day.'

He looked at me for a moment, and nodded. 'Good,' he said briefly.

The Fairy Wood was a large thicket of trees, many native, some obviously introduced a good many years ago with the apparent intention of attracting birds, and they had made this area more varied and dense than the natural, mostly eucalyptus, forest it joined. From it the view to the house was slightly downward and while I didn't feel the angle was one I would choose to use in a painting, I made suitably appreciative noises. Of course it wouldn't have mattered if the house had been an ugly red brick box built in a swamp: I would have declared myself eager to paint the scenery. As it was, I didn't have to pretend. Some of the angles of wall and trees and sky urged me to get out my sketching-pad. And to look down the valley, where narrow green fields were dotted with cattle, and a silver thread of water glinted in the sun as a little rocky stream chuckled between pale gold willows, and poplars stood, sentinels in yellow livery, guarding a bridge – the whole framed by forested hills – brought a lump to my throat in the way sheer beauty sometimes, absurdly and unexpectedly, does to me.

I think I had been standing for quite a little while, just looking, absorbed, before I recalled with a jolt that over this beauty a shadow hung on silent, perhaps dangerous wings.

Ivan was watching me when I turned and met his eyes, and he smiled as if understanding how the scene affected me. He said nothing and after a moment as we walked back towards the house, I said, 'I wish I could do it properly.'

'I think perhaps you will,' he said quietly. 'I have to admit I don't know anything about art, but I know there are all kinds of things you have to consider – light and shade and the best time of day, to begin with. So please feel free to come any time and as often as you wish. Maybe Vi and I might begin to learn a bit more about art if we see you at work.'

I laughed. 'I'm afraid you won't learn much from watching me. But it's very kind of you and I do appreciate it.'

Vi had returned to her book in the courtyard, and she put it aside to say pleasantly that she was glad I had found the place interesting enough to paint; when would I begin?

The phone rang and she got up rather quickly and went in to answer it. It seemed there was nothing more I could do, since Ivan had settled himself into a deck-chair and there seemed no chance Vi and I could have any conversation alone. So, saying I would probably come back tomorrow with my sketchbook, I left.

I had gained entree to the Norris household with absurd ease. But the next step – to gain Vi's confidence – could be very different.

Three

Next morning I phoned Miller's Plumbing and Draining and asked for Mr Miller.

'It's Lyn,' I told him when he picked up the phone with a cheerfully businesslike: 'Roger Miller. Can I help you?'

'And don't hang up,' I added quickly, 'because that's not going to do any good.'

'I'm afraid you have a wrong number,' he said coldly, but he didn't hang up immediately.

'I have no intention of going meekly away. We have to talk. You may as well give in and agree to meet me – here, at the place I'm renting: Lillian Ballard's place. Do you know where it is?'

'Look, lady, you're making a mistake. I tried to tell you that.'

'Do you know where Amber Cottage is – Miss Ballard's place?' I insisted.

'I explained –'

'*Do* you know where I'm staying?'

'Yes. But –'

'Then come and see me after work.' And I hung up before he could say anything more.

It was only eight o'clock in the morning, but I sat beside the phone with my head in my hands, feeling almost unbearably weary.

All my life, since the day he had walked out with two detectives, I had wanted to find my father, wanted to hear him say, 'Hey, kid!' – his own special greeting for me. Now I had found him – I was certain I had found him – and he wanted no part of knowing me. I could understand that he didn't want to be reminded of the prison years, but I wasn't part of those, surely. Why did he want to wipe out all the other years as well?

And as if that wasn't enough, I had – by proxy, as it were – been implored to help a mortally-afraid woman who now appeared to have neither need of help nor recollection of having asked for it.

Yet –

There had been something, some faint indefinable thing in the Norris household which had hovered on the fringe of my awareness and gave a hint of credence to that pleading letter. I had put it down to the fact that I was expecting something and my imagination had been prepared to create something accordingly. But now, in the cold light of a new day, I suddenly sat up with a jolt. One or both of the Norrises had been acting a part.

The more I thought of it, the more certain I was that it was so, though to save my life I couldn't have said why. I went carefully back in my memory over the previous afternoon, trying to recall exact words and, perhaps more importantly, voice inflections, gestures and all the things that have become known as body-language. And after a long time – which showed that either the acting had been good, or I had been particularly stupid – I understood.

They had been most welcoming and helpful. And they didn't want me there at all.

Neither of them?

I couldn't be certain about Ivan. Either he was a naturally outgoing person genuinely happy to have me setting up easels here and there about his garden, or he was the better actor. Curiously, I hoped he had been genuine.

But Vi, certainly, had not wanted me there. She had not wanted me to know it, but it was so. Because she had still hoped Lillian Ballard would come and I would be in the way of a private conversation? Perhaps I would be better able to judge that when I went out there again.

I spent the morning exploring the town on foot, principally because I wanted to shut the Norrises out of my mind, and physical exercise seemed the best antidote to an over-busied brain that was only functioning in unproductive circles. Some of the residential streets ran up quite steep hills and the effort of climbing them was rewarded with some delightful vistas over the town and, if one went far enough, over farmland and mountains beyond. There was a golf course over there, I noted. One day I might hire some clubs and play my own unpredictable brand of golf to help close my mind to its problems.

The local telephone directory had given an after-hours number for Miller's Plumbing, which matched the residential number of one of three R Millers listed, and it gave the residential address.

It was no coincidence that presently my walking exercise took me past a pleasant, comfortable-looking house in an unpretentious street – a white-painted house with a grey tile roof and blue trims on windows and doors, framed in a well-kept garden. A crab-apple red with tiny fruit, a few rhododendrons and a silver birch grew beside the footpath as if the house valued privacy but didn't want to totally shut the world out and hide behind a hedge of conifers or yew trees. It was hard not to stop and stare at my father's house and wonder whether he was happy there, and what it would have been like to live there with him and my mother, had things been different.

But things were not different, and after lunch I drove out again to the Norris house, armed this time with my sketch-book. I probably wouldn't even have given the motorcycle behind me a second thought, except that it *was* behind me and stayed behind me. Motorcycle riders are not usually noted for being content to stay behind a car which is being driven at a very moderate speed. Two or three other cars and one other motorcycle passed me on the sealed stretch of road, but that one bike stayed passively behind – not close, perhaps fifty metres was as close as it came: a red and white bike, its helmeted rider anonymous behind the helmet's face shield. I wondered if it would turn into the unsealed road which led to the Norris place, but when I turned the bike continued disinterestedly on its way, and I smiled ruefully at myself for getting so fanciful as to suspect I was being followed, though why I would be followed defied imagination.

Vi came to the front door in answer to the ring of the deep-toned bullock-bell which hung beside the solid timber door.

'Hello, Miss Sutton.' Her smile was immediate. Perhaps it was only the striking green eyes, which seemed to give such intensity to the way she looked at me, but I felt for a moment that she knew perfectly well that landscape painting was not my real reason for being here and she was fiercely concentrated on trying to fathom my motives. I hoped she might guess that I was here because, if she needed help, I was prepared to try to serve as Lillian Ballard's stand-in. It seemed absurd that I couldn't simply say: 'Look, I got your letter by mistake. Tell me what sort of help you need and I'll try to give it.'

But the letter had specifically forbidden that I – or Lillian – raise the subject: *Don't say anything to anyone – not even to me, not even if we are alone. That is very, very important.* I wished I knew why.

Certainly on my first visit there had been no chance for us to speak together without Ivan being there, but for the moment there was no sign of him.

I returned her smile and said cheerfully, 'Oh, call me Lyn, please. If I'm going to be poking around your garden with a pencil and a sketch-pad, let's not have awful formalities.'

'Good. My name's Vi.'

'Yes,' I said, 'I know.'

I saw suspicion leap into her eyes and I could have kicked myself. 'How did you know that?' She managed to make it sound a casual, half-amused query, but nothing concealed the relief in her face when I answered, 'I heard your husband call you that.'

'Oh, of course. Ivan's in town today – he goes in to his office two or three days a week, depending on appointments and banked-up work. He's a semi-retired accountant.'

This time I had more sense than to say I knew that also. 'I see. Have you lived here long?'

'About three years. Since Peter came to live with us. He's our foster-son.'

'Oh, yes, your husband mentioned him. He gave the Fairy Wood its name because of the fairy wrens. How old is he?' I had better not show I knew anything about Peter, either.

'Thirteen, nearly fourteen. He's very keen about birds and things. You're sure to meet him somewhere around the garden. He's in a wheelchair, but he gets about in it very well. Where would you like to sit to do your sketching? Do you need a chair or anything?'

I assured her I had everything I needed and had chosen a spot in the garden just in front of the house, where I could look down the valley.

'Sit on the verandah if you'd rather – you're welcome to make yourself as much at home as you like.'

I thanked her and before I could prolong the conversation she went back into the house, leaving me to reflect that if she wanted help she wasn't going to ask me for it. Her instant wariness on finding that I knew her name suggested she wondered, not whether I might be her friend, but whether I was her enemy. I sighed and tried to concentrate on my sketching, and indeed presently I became so absorbed in it that I could scarcely believe two hours had passed when Vi spoke beside me.

'I've made coffee, if you'd like to take a break, or shouldn't I interrupt when you're in the middle of sketching?'

'That's very kind of you – coffee would be most welcome and I've just about finished this sketch. These were a couple of false starts and I still haven't got it quite right, but I'm getting closer.' I showed her what I had done and she studied the work intently, then looked at me with a smile.

'I don't really know anything about it, but I think you're good.'

I laughed. 'Then there are certainly people who would

be happy to say that just *proves* you don't really know anything about it. But I hope you're right and they're wrong; and thank you. My work mightn't be very good yet, but I hope it will be some day.'

We sat comfortably in the little courtyard beside the house which trapped the autumn sun, and she asked why I preferred working with oils instead of watercolour, and where I came from in Queensland and why I'd chosen to come here to this area to paint.

'A friend told me once that it was a very attractive area – which it is – and it would give me a very different kind of landscape to try painting – which it does; so I decided to throw my hat over the windmill and give up my job and try to find out whether I can ever be an artist – though mind you I may well be looking for another job after a bit, because I'm afraid my savings will run out before I can make a living with a set of brushes – if I ever can. I was very lucky to find a cottage up for rent – a Miss Lillian Ballard's. Perhaps you know her?'

Vi gave me another searching look. 'Yes, I do,' she said noncommittally. Then after a moment's pause, 'Her cottage is up for rent?'

'Yes, I was most fortunate. The letting agent said Miss Ballard has gone overseas for six months or so. But no doubt you know that.'

'No, I didn't know. I haven't been in touch for quite some time.' Vi handed me coffee with a general air of lack of interest in Lillian's whereabouts. 'What's the next step in your painting?'

I wasn't prepared to abandon the subject of Lillian Ballard just yet. 'Oh, I'll make more sketches from different angles and then decide what I want to actually paint. I'm not sure what I should do about a couple of bits of mail that have come for Miss Ballard,' I said as if it were an afterthought.

'Take it back to the post office,' Vi advised. 'They're bound to have a forwarding address, or they can do the return-to-sender bit.'

'Actually there's one letter not even addressed – just

pushed into the letter-box,' I half-lied. 'It's in a sealed envelope so I don't like to open it.'

Vi passed me a sandwich. 'Some junk mail, I should imagine. Toss it in the garbage if you don't want to open it.'

All I could detect was indifference. No concern, no agitation, nothing to suggest someone fearful of being murdered. Except that strange, intense watchfulness with which she regarded me. If I had nurtured any thought of being a female version of a knight in shining armour rushing to the rescue of a damsel in distress, I could forget it for the present. Unless she was mentally unhinged in a way which only occasionally manifested itself, there was some reason why Vi would trust only Lillian Ballard. And Lillian was on the far side of the world tramping through spring fields in Norway. I hope you get chilblains, I thought unkindly; why the dickens did you have to go off just now and leave me with this mess?

'This mess' consisting of a striking-looking woman in early middle age who was either schizophrenic or in peril for her life, and who was now offering me a second cup of coffee as if the principal concern in her life was showing hospitality to a wandering artist.

I had said my farewell to Vi, saying I would probably be back again next day if the weather was sunny, and was just putting my sketching gear away when a woman's voice beside me said, 'Hello. You're the artist, then?'

I turned quickly. A small, frail-looking grey-haired lady in her early seventies was watching me with alert blue eyes behind silver-rimmed glasses.

'Hello. Yes, I'm Lyn Sutton.' And who on earth are you? I wondered.

'Sutton, is it?' She seemed to ponder that for a moment. 'Not a friend of theirs, are you?' She nodded towards the house.

'No. That is, I hadn't met Mr and Mrs Norris until yesterday. They've kindly allowed me to come here to do some painting. It's very picturesque.'

'Yes.' Whether that was agreement that the scenery was

appealing or whether it was indicative she knew why I was here, I didn't know. 'I didn't think you were a friend of theirs.'

I didn't know quite what to make of that, either. I smiled politely. 'Do you live here, Mrs –?'

'Wishart. They haven't mentioned me, eh? But they will: Aunt Edith's a bit eccentric, they'll say. It sounds better than saying Aunt Edith's a drunk.'

I blinked and managed some sort of a smile.

'I have what they call a granny-flat, you know the sort of thing: a place to eat, a place to sleep, and your own plumbing set-up. Only mine's separate and bigger than most, and so it should be. It's rather nice. I still drive my own car and I can drive a lot better than half the young idiots who think they're ready for Le Mans when they should still be riding tricycles for all the brains they've got. Oh, don't worry, I only drive when I'm sober.'

She laughed and the laughter was so unexpectedly joyful and real that I joined in, automatically liking Edith Wishart but understanding that Vi could hardly turn to her as a reliable ally.

'So,' she said, 'you've come to paint the scenery. Do you do portraits as well?'

'I'm afraid not.'

'Just as well. Just as well. Portrait painters are supposed to be able to capture the soul of the subject or something aren't they? You could get some very strange results around here.'

She went off chuckling, but the amusement was no longer outgoing innocence and I was left staring after her.

I had vaguely registered the sound of a car driving up, but I jumped slightly when Ivan said, behind me, 'What was Aunt Edith talking about?'

I turned. 'I think she wanted me to paint her portrait. She asked if I did portraits.'

Ivan raised an eyebrow and laughed, accepting the story with – I thought – a touch of relief.

'Take no notice of Aunt Edith. She's sharp enough in some ways, but very rambling in others, especially at times.

She hasn't any family except us, so she has her own cottage here and is quite comfortable and independent. She's well able to look after herself, but she's a shade –' He hesitated.

'Eccentric?' I suggested.

'You could say that.'

We looked at each other and smiled.

'She was married to my mother's brother and she's welcome to have a home with us as long as she chooses,' he added.

I remembered Edith Wishart had said her granny-flat was bigger than most 'and so it should be,' and I wondered whether giving her a home had not been purely a charitable family gesture.

It was a few days later and I was just beginning to prepare my evening meal when the doorbell rang and Roger Miller was standing on the doorstep, evidently having come straight from work. Before I could say a word he strode into the house, pulled the door away from my hand and shut it.

'Are you alone here?' he demanded.

'Yes. I'm glad you –'

'You wanted to talk,' he cut in curtly. 'Clearly you're going to continue making a damned nuisance of yourself until you get this thing straight, so I'm here. So talk.'

'Let's at least sit down.' I was trying to sort out a jumble of thoughts, wishing I'd known he was coming.

He sat in one of Lillian Ballard's easy chairs by the fire and I sat in another, and he looked at me with flint-hard eyes and a face devoid of expression, and I felt incredibly nervous. This was my only chance, I thought; if I got it wrong now, Roger was gone from me for keeps. He would never talk – really talk – to me; never let me get to know him. And right now, after all the months – years – I had planned this, I had no idea what to say. It was like having studied and rehearsed for one play, and then on opening night being told you were playing in a different one, and you'd just have to take your cues from the other players and improvise, with only the sketchiest idea of the story-line.

'Perhaps,' I said, 'we can best begin by being honest.

You're Roger Sutton, and my father.'

'I'm Roger Miller and you had better remember it.'

'Very well. You're Roger Miller. But you were born Sutton and you're my father. When I called you Mr Sutton out in the yard behind your shop the other day, you reacted before you could stop yourself, because I caught you off guard. I knew where to find you; I knew you'd changed your name to Miller; I know you married a widow with two teenage children. It cost me quite a lot of money to find that out, so please let's stop pretending.'

He was leaning forward in his chair and for several seconds he just sat motionless, staring at me. 'What do you want?' he demanded.

'I want to get to know you. I *need* to get to know you, to know the sort of person you are now – not my little-girl's image of what you were, not the image the old newspaper stories create. I need to know you so that I can know better what sort of person I am.'

He hadn't taken his eyes off me, and the hostility in them hadn't lessened. 'That's rubbish. You are yourself. You're not your father, nor your mother, your grandparents or anyone else. You're what you make of yourself. Don't ask your ancestors to accept responsibility for you.'

'That's perfectly true, but we all carry some of our ancestors' genes. All right, maybe I shouldn't care. My life would be more comfortable if I didn't, but I do care. I just want to get to know you a little. I'd like you to tell me about the robbery – the truth – but that's not as important as getting to know about your present life.'

He laughed sneeringly. 'Good God, did you come here as some sort of soap-opera heroine to prove my innocence after all these years? Have you got some adolescent dream of newspaper headlines: Devoted Daughter Clears Father's Name – or some such tripe?'

'No,' I answered levelly. 'I knew a long time ago that you were guilty. I read the old newspapers. I read the transcript of the trial. My father was a thief; he may have been a murderer. What I want to know is this: what is he now? And why did he do what he did nearly twenty years ago?'

Those dark eyes were unwaveringly cold. 'Go home,' he said bitterly. 'Go back to your nice comfortable safe life and leave the real world alone.'

'The real world!' Anger suddenly erupted in me as I thought of all the years when Roger Sutton's past had haunted me. 'Real! I'll tell you what the real world is like for the families of people like you. It's seeing your mother grow grim and silent; it's moving on in case someone finds out who you are. It's being taunted by the other kids in school when they *do* find out. It's being scared to fill out job application forms when they want to know your father's name – in case someone remembers, or they check it out. And when you have a job, it's being afraid someone, some day, somehow, is going to find out you've got criminal blood and they wonder if you can be trusted around the petty-cash box and maybe someone else should do the banking. It's feeling you have to tell –'

I stopped.

It had been feeling, two years ago, I had to tell Eric before I married him. It had been feeling his arms go loose around me. Hearing him say it didn't make any difference, in a stunned voice; knowing that it did – it made a hell of a difference to a young solicitor on his way up. It had been a phone call to tell me he'd been offered this great position in Perth – too good to turn down – and as soon as he was settled he'd be in touch. It had been hanging up the phone, fumbling with the hurting because you knew he'd never be in touch.

Well, it had been two years. I looked up from my clenched hands to see Roger still watching me, but with a different expression. 'Men?' he asked quietly.

'*A* man. Yes.' I swallowed hard. 'I want to hear about that night from you.'

His face was blankly hard again. 'If you've read the transcript of the trial you know all there is to know. I've nothing to add to that. Just go home.'

'No. Not till I get to know you better.'

'*Listen* to me, will you? You had better go home. Get out of this town. What I did, I did. I can't change it. I spent twelve years behind walls for it. I've worked myself into the ground to build a new life, but I've built it. And before God, you had better not wreck it.'

'I'm not here to wreck anything. What are you talking about?'

He said menacingly, 'Do you have any idea what twelve years of prison are like? What they can do to a man? I'm not the father you remember from when you were little. He doesn't exist. But Roger Miller does. I have a business that's small but solid, and it's scrupulously straight. I'm clean. Not because I've turned saintly, but because I've got sensible. I have a wife I love, two step-children I'm very fond of and who, I flatter myself, have accepted me as being OK. I am not going to have you hanging around to cost me any of that.'

I asked sharply, 'Don't your wife and her children *know*?'

'No. And they're not going to. Do I make myself clear?'

'I shan't tell them, I assure you. But, Dad –'

He leapt up as the word slipped from me automatically. 'Don't you call me that! *Ever.*'

His cold fury was real, and almost frightening, but I knew I must refuse to be cowed, because that was what he wanted. I was fully aware that he was trying to frighten me.

'What am I to call you, then?' I asked mildly.

'Not worthwhile calling me anything, because beyond this evening we won't be seeing each other.'

'Then I'll call you Roger. And you're wrong, you know. About your wife and step-children. Things have a way of getting known –'

'If you're planning a bit of blackmail, forget it or you'll disappear in Blowering Dam or some other convenient spot.' His voice was glass-cutting hard.

'I'm not planning blackmail. Have a grain of sense. And you don't frighten me, you know.'

He stared at me for a long moment and then finally nodded. 'No, I don't, do I?' He sat down again. 'Why?' He sounded genuinely curious.

'You're my father. I adored you. Nothing would ever convince me you'd harm me.'

'Even if I killed a nightwatchman?'

'Did you?'

His eyes narrowed. 'Beyond a reasonable doubt.'

'That doesn't answer me.'

He was silent for a little while. 'Is that why you came here? To ask me that question?'

It was my turn to stare silently at the fire for a few moments. 'In the end,' I said slowly, 'yes, I suppose it is.'

'Then it was a wasted exercise. Because unless I break down and confess, which I'm not going to, I can deny it till this time next year and you still won't know if it's the truth.'

'That's what Mother said,' I said without thinking.

He gave a short laugh. 'Then she has more sense than you have.'

He stood up and moved towards the door, and I stood also.

'You can walk away,' I told him, 'but you haven't finished with me. I don't give up that easily.'

He turned on me. 'I'll tell you once more, and this time *listen*. Stay out of my life.'

'Your life! What about mine? You had a wife and child, and nothing can wipe that out, nothing in all eternity. Don't you ever think about what you did to *our* lives? Very well, I'll tell *you* once more: all I want is a chance to get to know you, to form my own opinion of what sort of man you are; that's all. I think you owe me that much.'

He walked out without a word.

Four

It was in a thoroughly dispirited frame of mind that I drove out to the Norris house again. It seemed I was getting absolutely nowhere. My father didn't want to know I existed and it certainly seemed Vi Norris's frantic plea for help had been written in a moment of now-forgotten hysteria. I wondered about Alzheimer's disease, that often premature process of ageing in which the brain can play many tricks, often unkindly. But there was nothing in what I could see of Vi's behaviour which suggested she was a victim.

I'd had a dream the previous night – a near-nightmare brought on, no doubt, by the situation I'd managed to get myself into. I had been in a brick-walled enclosure which had no roof, but no windows or doors, and the walls were far too high for me to reach the top. I had pounded futilely on the featureless walls in growing panic because there was no way out, and suddenly the walls had become hedges, trimmed and angular, and I had realized I was in a maze and instead of hopeless imprisonment there was a way out, if only I could find it.

My dream had faded then without showing me the way out of the maze, but evidently my sleeping brain was trying to reassure itself. But the feeling of optimism which had come in my dream had deserted me before I even began to chat with Vi and, while she was as polite as ever, and entirely pleasant, she clearly had no wish to discuss anything as confidential as prospective murder.

As a substitute for Lillian Ballard I was clearly no great shakes.

Vi retreated into the house and as I set up my easel I suddenly remembered the motorcycle. I hadn't really thought about it at the time, but it had been behind me again this morning as I drove out from town. The same bike? I frowned, trying to remember. I couldn't be certain, but I thought so. It had been further behind me this time and as I'd neared the Norrises' turn-off it had accelerated past. It must have been nothing but coincidence and only a jumpy mind was attaching any importance to it.

Again, when I began work I became absorbed in it and I could not have said how long I'd been working when I heard a soft hiss like bicycle tyres on the concrete path behind me and I turned.

A pale, dark-haired boy of thirteen or fourteen was regarding me with intent brown eyes. A bit above average height, he had a slim wiry build which hinted at strength and held the promise of athletic development; but for the wheelchair.

'Hello,' I said. 'You must be Peter. I'm Lyn.'

He nodded. 'Vi told me. Hello. Mind if I watch for a bit? I can keep quiet.'

I smiled, looking at him. I just bet you can keep quiet, I thought. There was something about him which said this boy was a loner. Maybe that had only come about since he'd been stuck in a wheelchair; maybe he didn't get much company outside this household.

'I don't mind if you watch,' I told him. 'And I don't mind if you talk a bit, either.'

A nice-looking boy,. his black hair and pale olive skin suggesting something Mediterranean in his background – Italian, I thought, but maybe Greek.

'How come you're not at school?' I asked.

'The schools around here have steps,' he said curtly. 'I do correspondence lessons.'

He evidently thought I was pretending not to notice the chair. 'That's a pity,' I said. 'I would have thought most schools these days would make provisions for students in wheelchairs.'

'Not here.'

He was watching me mix paint, his face intent.

'I see,' I said.

He was silent for a long time, keeping his promise not to chatter. When I glanced around at him again he wasn't watching what I was doing. He was watching me, with those dark brown eyes, and his gaze was oddly disconcerting, as if he were trying to assess me. This, I thought, would not be an easy boy to get to know, but the intelligent, watchful face suggested that getting to know what went on behind the dark eyes might be interesting. I am often puzzled by whatever it is that sometimes makes one person react to another almost on the moment of meeting – a reaction of immediate liking or disliking, and for no apparent reason. I felt it strongly with this boy who was barely more than a child. I liked Peter, rightly or wrongly.

Whether or not he liked me, I couldn't even guess.

I tried asking him about his studies – which year of high-school he was in, what were his favourite subjects. He answered courteously enough, but in monosyllables where possible.

'I'm afraid I wasn't very studious,' I confessed cheerfully, leaning back to look at the light on a cloud I wasn't capturing well enough. 'Maths was my worst subject, hotly followed by science, which I soon gave up in favour of history. If they'd allowed it I'd have dropped maths in kindergarten.'

He gave me the flicker of a smile, having just told me, under questioning, that maths and science were his best subjects.

'Do you like reading, or are you a TV watcher?'

'I read a lot.'

'Have you ever tried to paint?'

'Not really. A bit, not much.'

Mainly for something to say, but partly because I felt it might be true, I said, 'I've a feeling you might be rather good at it.'

He shrugged. 'I'd rather take photographs.'

Something in the way he said it made it sound important to him.

'Well,' I said, 'that's certainly a form of art. Do you take any particular sort of photographs?'

For a moment his face came alive. 'I'm going to be the best wildlife photographer in the world!' Then on the instant his face froze. 'Or I *was* going to be.'

And he dexterously spun his wheelchair around and wheeled violently away, head bent, just as Ivan and another man came out of the house.

Watching the boy's retreating form, Ivan said quietly, 'I'm sorry if Peter was rude to you. I'm afraid he's a bit moody these days. He wasn't always like that.'

I shook my head. 'He wasn't rude at all. And if he finds life sometimes very hard to take, it's hardly surprising.'

'No, I guess not. At first the doctors thought he would walk again, but now it seems quite hopeless – more damage done than they realized.'

His face had been very serious as he watched Peter, but now he turned and smiled. 'Lyn, this is Arnold Bright, a friend of ours. Arnold's a teacher, and he comes out a couple of afternoons a week to help Peter with his high-school subjects.'

Arnold Bright was a tall thin man of about forty, with slightly-receding mid-fair hair and alert grey eyes behind rimless glasses. We shook hands and he said, 'And the reason I'm not in a classroom dispensing gems of knowledge on what should be a working day can be explained by a mild attack of the industrial-dispute syndrome. The Teachers' Union called a one-day strike over the size of classes. I'm delighted to meet you.' What was otherwise a fairly unremarkable face was transformed by a smile which made this serious-looking teacher suddenly look charmingly mischievous.

'Will you both excuse me?' Ivan said. 'I have to meet a client at the office.'

With a quick wave of his hand he hurried out to his car. Arnold Bright said, 'It's hard on him and Vi. Peter, I mean. They blame themselves for his accident. And the truth is, I was partly to blame as well.'

I looked at him. 'I'm sorry,' I said, 'I don't know what

happened to Peter.'

'Oh.' He sat down on the grass beside the little folding chair I use when I'm painting, his knees drawn up and arms around them.

'I got to know Ivan and Vi through caving – you know, exploring caves – speleology. Vi belongs to a local club and I joined it when I came here a couple of years ago. There are a couple of unexplored caves on Mt Bartholomew, which is only a twenty-minute drive from here – or a two-hour walk if you know the short-cut through the bush. The cave entrances are both on next-to-inaccessible faces of the mountain, nowhere near the bottom. There's no road anywhere near to get there from the bottom, anyway, but if you're any good at rock-climbing you can get down from the top. The one on the east face isn't too difficult at all – dead easy if you use ropes, and Vi and I have been down to it several times, but at that time we hadn't got far in. We had a theory – still have, for that matter, though we've never proved it – that this cave may be linked to the one on the south face.'

He had picked up a pebble and was turning it over in his fingers – like someone fingering worry-beads, I thought.

'The south face is not for amateurs, in my opinion, ropes or no ropes. It's much closer to sheer, and there are long drops if you miss your footing, but it's no problem to an experienced abseiler, and both Vi and I are pretty experienced. So this day we'd arranged to go down to the cave entrance to follow our theory that the two caves are in fact one, with two entrances. I guess you could say it was an ego thing: we wanted to be able to go to the other members and say "Look what we found" – because even the existence of the caves isn't widely known.

'Peter wanted to come with us, as he often did. He's done some climbing and caving, too, but in much safer places. Vi agreed he could come but not climb, which he accepted. He had his camera and he was going to look for birds to photograph while we went down to the south-face cave – we reckoned to be away about four hours. Peter and I were getting the gear out of the car while Vi looked for good anchor-points for the ropes we'd have to use to go down the cliff, and Vi caught her foot between two rocks and stumbled and fell, spraining her ankle. Obviously she couldn't do any climbing or caving that day, so I'd have simply come home, but Vi didn't want to spoil the day completely, so she suggested Peter take her place. He was delighted, of course, and as he said, he really was quite good on the rocks, and was ready for something a bit more difficult than Ivan and Vi had allowed him to do up till then.'

He was still turning the pebble over and over, looking at it and seeing what had happened that day at the cliff.

'I was quite prepared to take him, but not on the south face because I thought it was too tough for him – too dangerous. So we switched to the east face. I had my own rope and harness, Peter had Vi's. As we abseiled down one of the sections where you have to rely entirely on the rope, Peter's rope broke.'

'*Broke?* With *Peter's* weight?' I was incredulous.

He nodded, his face stony. 'Vi keeps her climbing and caving gear in the shed.' He nodded at a large workshop-cum-storage shed at the back of the house and a little distant from it. 'Ivan had put an old car-battery on the shelf above, and at some stage it had been knocked over and the battery-acid had spilled down on to the coil of climbing rope. It's highly corrosive stuff, as you know, and it's good at chewing holes in fabric. There wasn't any frightfully obvious damage to the rope, and Vi had already taken it out of the car when she sprained her ankle, and in the confusion no one checked it. But when weight was put on it the damaged rope simply gave way, and Peter fell.'

He flung the pebble away savagely. 'If it had been on the south face he'd have been killed. It was on the east face where I thought he'd be safe, and he's stuck in a wheelchair.'

After a moment I said gently, 'It wasn't your fault that he fell. And by taking the precautions you did, you saved his life.'

'For what it's worth. It's hard on both Ivan and Vi. They

both blame themselves – Vi for not checking the rope and Ivan for not noticing the battery had been knocked over; and for putting it there in the first place. Peter wasn't like us,' he added. 'He didn't want to learn climbing and caving for the sake of climbing and caving. They were skills needed in his plans for a career.'

'As a wildlife photographer. The best in the world.' I was filled with sadness for the dark-eyed boy who had seen his dream so terribly shattered.

'He told you?' Arnold Bright looked at me quickly.

I nodded.

'It wasn't just a childhood fancy,' Arnold said. 'Peter's very mature for his years. Being a wildlife photographer was a deep-rooted passion. And I believe he'd have made the grade. Try to get him to show you some of his photographs some day.'

We were both silent for a while. I felt a warm respect for this quietly-spoken man who was filled with compassion for Peter. I had forgotten about painting and just sat, looking down the valley but seeing in my mind a boy on a smooth sheer sheet of rock, trusting to a rope whose strands were rotten.

Then a thought began to grow disturbingly in my mind.

Peter had met with Vi's accident.

It was Vi's rope, Vi's harness, and it was only due to chance that it was not Vi who was using them. *I am going to be killed*, the note had said. *It will look like an accident, but it will be murder*.

Peter would have been killed if the rope had broken on a climb down the south face of the mountain, Arnold had said. Vi would have been climbing on the south face. She would have been killed. And it would have looked like an accident. Would it have been an accident?

Was it simply that the realization of how near she had come to falling to her death had sparked Vi's fears? Had the whole incident grown in her mind until it became a deep-rooted fear, an obsession? And had something else happened, more recently, to confirm her fears, at least in her own mind?

I wondered if she suspected someone in particular, and if so, was it Ivan she feared? I found that hard to imagine. She certainly displayed no uneasiness in his company. If she had no suspect, only suspicion, she must live a very hard life, fearful of lurking peril and having no idea where the danger lay.

Although Ivan accepted that the blame for the spilled battery-acid lay in his carelessness, he might be blaming himself wrongly. If the damage to the rope had been deliberate, anyone – even a total outsider – could have caused it. Probably the shed where Vi's climbing equipment was kept wasn't locked, and it wasn't so close to the house that entry unobserved would be especially difficult.

I was so absorbed in my thoughts I had forgotten Arnold Bright. I gave a little start when he presently said, 'Your being here might be very good for Peter. He might be encouraged to take up painting instead of photography. There's no question he's very artistic, and perhaps if he could portray some of his beloved birds and possums and things in oils instead of on film, it might give him some sort of consolation.'

'Well, I've only just met him. I rather think he told me that painting wasn't for him. But of course I'll be happy to try to get him interested, if you think it would help.'

'Even apart from that angle, he doesn't get to see enough people. A bit of new company would be healthy. Now I'd better go and see how he's making out with his English assignment.' He stood up and smiled at me, then walked away.

I found it hard to think of him doing a dare-devil rock-climb or wading through underground streams and crawling over bruising rocks deep in a night-black cave. Appearances, clearly, could be deceptive.

It was difficult to concentrate on my painting, but I struggled on for a while. Ivan came back presently, waving to me as he went into the house. I decided it was no use trying to persist with my work, at least for the moment. Thinking perhaps a walk would clear my thoughts and let me settle down to brushes and oils again and fix my mind on what my eyes were seeing instead of what my brain was picturing, I walked up to the Fairy Wood. There were less-than-mouse-sized wrens skipping through the grasses, perching sometimes on a single grass seed-stem without more than gently bending it. There were magpies and crimson rosellas and fly-catchers and others I couldn't recognize. I might get Peter to identify them for me, I thought; that would be better than looking them up in my bird-book. After a while the peace of the place, the pleasure of watching the birds – even if I wasn't on name-terms with them – began to quieten my rattled thoughts and I walked back towards the house.

My glance fell on the shed and I diverted to it. I should be unobserved from the house and I'd like to know whether it was locked, because if it wasn't locked now the chances were it never had been locked, which meant that anyone, but anyone, could have sabotaged Vi's climbing rope. If anyone had ever dreamed of doing so.

The shed in fact had two doors, one fastened by a pad-bolt which could conceivably be secured by a padlock but which certainly wasn't at the moment, and the second door fastened with a large but simple barrel bolt which didn't lend itself to padlocks. So the shed was open to anyone who cared to enter, and it always had been. I walked on towards the house and as I approached I heard voices from the back garden. Eavesdropping wasn't high on my list of vices, but something in the tone of Vi's voice caught my attention. I didn't hear what she said, but Ivan answered in the tone someone might use to calm another person's unreasonable fears.

'I tell you it's all right,' he said. 'She doesn't constitute any kind of problem. How could she?'

'I don't like it,' Vi said tautly. 'She's dangerous, no matter what you say.'

Ivan laughed. 'Nonsense! What on earth put that idea in your head? It's all right, I promise you.'

They moved away and I heard no more.

But the note had said Ivan would make a joke of Vi's

conviction she was going to be murdered. Well, Ivan had just made a joke of something that was worrying Vi.

She's dangerous, Vi had said. She. Who? Me? Hardly; she'd never set eyes on me when she sat down to type that panic-stricken note. But then, if she had some kind of recurring phobia in which she repeatedly imagined someone was trying to kill her, the earlier fear might have evaporated and now had been replaced by an imagined danger from a new source – this time, me.

I still found it very hard to believe there was anything wrong with Vi's mind, though I was also aware that in many cases of schizophrenia and other mental problems it was exceedingly difficult for even a psychiatrist to identify the problem or notice that there was one.

So assuming Vi was not mentally or emotionally unbalanced, it was not Ivan she feared, and not me. Then who was 'she'? Aunt Edith? It was a bit absurd to regard a frail-looking seventy-year-old as a danger. It wasn't Lillian Ballard, because she was supposed to receive the plea for help. But of course – the thought suddenly occurred to me – the danger Vi referred to might not be a physical danger at all. The person they were discussing might be involved in business dealings or even in a sporting event as totally removed as the American Open Women's tennis tournament, or 'she' might be a mare in a horse-race they were proposing to bet on. I was prepared to attach too much significance to the word 'danger' in my present frame of mind.

I ran my fingers impatiently through my hair and sighed as I walked back towards where my easel stood waiting. There was no way I could concentrate my brain on any more painting today.

'You look,' said a voice beside me, 'as if you have more worries than you can deal with.'

I swung around, startled. Edith Wishart stood in a doorway, regarding me with a twinkle in her eyes. 'Come and have a cup of tea with me,' she said.

Mrs Wishart's 'flat' was in fact a separate cottage up the hill a little toward Peter's Fairy Wood, and was joined to the main house by a covered walkway. It was tastefully and comfortably furnished and the car which stood outside was a Peugeot a few years old but in fine condition. Aunt Edith, I gathered, was not wealthy, but by no means the poor relation either.

'It's very nice for me to have a bit of company,' she said as she made tea and put out home-made fruit-cake. 'Peter often used to come and have tea with me after he came home from school, and we'd play backgammon or mah-jong, but he doesn't come any more.'

'It's very sad to see a boy like that confined to a wheelchair,' I said, feeling stupidly that that was the sort of banal obvious remark everyone made, but I couldn't think what else to say.

'Peter's changed.' Mrs Wishart shook her head as if puzzled.

'I guess when you have your life turned upside down in a few seconds it's inevitable it must have a pretty profound psychological effect as well as the physical one,' I suggested gently.

She nodded sadly. 'It's something very hard for anyone to cope with, and Peter had set his heart on being a wildlife photographer and that's all gone now. But I wish – I wish he wouldn't shut everyone out.'

I glanced at her. Edith Wishart might be an alcoholic; she might be eccentric as well, but she was totally in charge of her brain right now. There was no trace of the erratic behaviour I'd seen in her at our first meeting. I wondered if I could steer the conversation to Vi, to try to ascertain if there was some psychotic problem that was known about.

'It must put a great strain on Vi and Ivan,' I said. 'Especially Vi. It wouldn't be awfully surprising if her nerves were in tatters.' It wasn't a very subtle approach.

Neither was the reply. 'I don't see any signs of it,' Mrs Wishart said.

'Arnold Bright told me something of Peter's accident. He said Vi and Ivan both blame themselves for the rope breaking.'

'Very hard to sensibly attach blame in that sort of

accident. If an accident is genuinely an accident there's no point in dwelling on it. Though I think –'

She stopped. 'More tea?' she asked, and then firmly led the conversation into other channels. It was only later that she mentioned Peter again, and that was not in relation to the accident.

'I've lived here for a long time,' she said when talk had revolved around my home in Queensland. 'My husband used to enjoy trout-fishing, so when he retired he wanted to move here from Sydney, because he'd often fished in this area and loved it. He liked this place – it had been a sheep farm but a lot of the land had been sold off, and he liked the idea of having enough property to still run a few sheep for a hobby, plus which there's a nice stretch of trout stream. When he died a few years ago I didn't want to leave, but the house was too big and I could simply not cope with the property. We had no family and Ivan was really my only relative and I knew he was semi-retired in Melbourne, so I offered them the property for a good deal less than its value, provided I could live on here for the rest of my days by building this cottage. Then of course when Peter's mother was killed he had no one so he came here, too.'

'So it all worked out very well,' I said.

'Yes,' she said, and somehow it seemed to me she meant 'no.'

I looked at her quickly. She was looking down at her plate but her mind was clearly somewhere else and her face was troubled.

She looked up and met my eyes. 'And now Peter's crippled,' she said flatly. 'Strange how things work out, isn't it? If I'd sold this place to strangers, Ivan and Vi would still be living in Melbourne and Peter would still be walking.'

'You can't blame yourself for that!' I protested.

'No,' she said slowly. 'But sometimes you wonder how much is the hand of God and how much is the hand of man. Will you excuse me a moment? My tea's cold. I'll just get some hot water in my cup.'

She went out to the kitchen and when she came back a few minutes later she smelled strongly of brandy and I rather thought that what she had poured into her teacup was not hot water.

To make conversation I said, 'So Peter is – what relation to you? A great-nephew?'

'He's not related to me at all, really, and actually only a fairly distant relation of Vi's. He's the son of her cousin Elaine who never got around to marrying Peter's father – or more accurately he never got around to marrying her. He lived in the fast lane, as they say, and family ties weren't his scene. They lived together a couple of years, even after Peter was born, as I understand it. Then he was inconsiderate enough to get himself killed in one of those micro aircraft. Elaine hadn't anyone, but she had a good job and she coped with Peter on her own till a semi-trailer failed to take a corner one morning while she was driving her car to work, and Peter was left without a soul to care about what happened to him. So as Vi was Elaine's nearest – and I think probably only – relative, she and Ivan took Peter in.'

'That was very kind of them,' I commented.

She looked at me for a second, her eyes bright with the first intake of alcohol, before it began to dull eye and brain. 'Oh, yes,' she said. 'Very kind.' She frowned. 'And now they're too kind.'

I raised an eyebrow. 'Too kind?'

'They want to wrap him in cotton-wool, treat him as if he was some delicate piece of fragile bone-china. But he isn't. He's a teenage boy, not a Dresden doll.' She drank from her teacup. 'It's wrong,' she said, and shook her head as if something was puzzling her.

'Next time you come,' she said brightly, 'we must play backgammon.'

I smiled, thanked her for the tea, and left.

Just about the junction of the Norris road and the main road a red and white motorcycle was pulled off to the side of the road and the man who had delivered Vi's note was squatted on his haunches tinkering with some of the machine's presumably vital parts.

Twice, probably three times, a machine like that had been behind my car when I drove out. It was absurd to think I was being followed, but I was at least curious, and I didn't feel threatened by this anonymous bike-rider. If he had intended to harm me he could have done so long since.

I stopped my car beside him. 'Having trouble?'

He looked up. 'No, it's all right, thank you – nothing disastrous and it's fixed. Oh, hello – you're the lady from Amber Cottage.'

'You're surprised to see me?' There was probably a touch of sarcasm in my voice.

He shrugged and stood up. He was above average height, trim and muscular, with wavy blond hair – not handsome, certainly, but a pleasant-looking fellow of about thirty. 'Well, I suppose it's a fairly small town.'

'And since you've been following me, meeting me should be even less surprising. Would you mind explaining?' I hadn't meant to accuse him of following me, because logically I couldn't be certain; but, illogically, I was.

'*Following* you? Look, I'm here on holiday and I've been riding around looking at the scenery and doing a bit of fishing. Sure, you may have seen me. But I'm not the kind of perv that snoops after women.' There was a hint of anger in his voice. Then, looking at me hard, he said, 'Why do you think someone was following you?'

'Several times there's been a motorcycle behind my car – I don't know anything about bikes, but the one I've seen is red and white like yours.'

He smiled. 'Oh, I see. There are quite a few machines like this around. I hired mine from Galbraith's Garage, and all their bikes are like this. A Yamaha behind you four times is probably four different Yamahas. Nothing to worry about. Have you lived here long?'

He seemed to think he'd solved the question of the following motorbike, and probably he had, at least to his satisfaction.

'I don't live here. I'm on holiday. I'm just renting the cottage.'

'Family holiday, I suppose. That's why you have the cottage?'

'No family. Only me.' I wasn't sure why I was telling him anything, except that I felt friendless and alone with a heap of problems. Lines from a poem of wartime Britain came into my head, about an American girl alone at a ball who is mistaken by an Englishman for someone he is supposed to meet:

I meant to tell him, but changed my mind.
I needed a friend, and he seemed kind.

'You see,' I added, 'I paint landscapes, and this seems to me an attractive area.' I had not really meant to volunteer this information, either.

'Are you – pardon my ignorance – an established painter or purely a recreational artist? Pictures in art galleries – that sort of thing – or just for fun?'

'A few in art galleries. Oh, not the big public galleries that buy things to put on display. A couple of galleries that sell on commission. They haven't sold many yet,' I added with a rueful smile.

'Give it time,' he said seriously. 'I don't know anything about art – though like most people I know what I like. I'm afraid my tastes are pretty conventional for the most part. Is that what you were doing up there?' He nodded at the road I had just driven down. 'Painting?'

'Yes. Some people named Norris are kindly letting me paint the view down the valley from their house.'

The dark blue eyes were studying me. He smiled, almost as if he'd reached some kind of decision. 'Pardon my bad manners. I should have introduced myself. My name's Liam Stuart. I'm awfully sorry if I *have* been riding behind your car once or twice and making you worry that you were being followed. If it did happen I promise it wasn't intentional. May I make amends by taking you to dinner tonight? Not on this,' He added with a disarming widening of his smile. 'I only hired this because I like riding bikes. I do have a car. Will you come?'

I heard myself say I'd like to, and to my surprise I meant it. 'I can't, though; not tonight.'

I had phoned Roger to ask him to come to see me. I didn't expect he would come, but I didn't dare risk not being there, just in case he did.

'Tomorrow night?'

'Thank you. Yes.'

'Good. And,' with a twinkle, 'may I know who I'm taking to dinner?'

I laughed. It was the first time in quite a few days that I had laughed so easily and with real amusement. 'Sorry. Lyndal Sutton. Everyone calls me Lyn.'

A strange expression flickered across his face for just a second, and then the smile was back. 'Then I'll call for you about seven tomorrow evening, Lyn.' He slipped his motorcyclist's helmet on, gave me a cheery wave, and roared off towards town. I started my car again and followed at a more sedate pace, and as I drove, the next two lines of Alice Duer-Miller's story-in-verse came unbidden into my mind:

So I put my gloved hand into his glove,
And we danced together – and fell in love.

With a smile I pushed the thought impatiently away. Had I imagined the momentary look of something almost like shock Liam Stuart had registered on hearing my name? He couldn't have heard of me, so the name must have reminded him of something out of his past – something which hurt.

The thought was still weaving its way among a good many other thoughts about the day's events while I was putting away my painting equipment. I paused for a moment to study the partly-done painting with a critical eye. The *light*, I thought. That was the vital thing. That was what made landscapes. I had to get the light right; the thread of light that was the distant trout-stream, the filtered light through the golden elm leaves, the variants in the clouds. I was thinking of that when Roger Miller came to the door.

Although I had faintly hoped he might come I found it hard to hide my astonishment that he had. 'Hello, Roger,' I said in an attempt at an unsurprised-sounding greeting.

'Come in. Sorry I'm late with coffee, but I was out a bit longer than I intended.'

'Don't bother about coffee. I had some earlier.' He glanced at the fireplace. 'Do you want your fire lit?'

My heart leapt. This man with the whip-tough body and the spirit hardened into steel by all the fearsome things twelve years of prison can do, was behaving like any normal father on a casual visit to his daughter. He must have gone home after work because obviously he'd showered and changed. 'Can I get you a drink, then? I'm afraid I haven't a very extensive cellar. Sherry? Scotch?'

'Scotch and water, thanks.'

When I came back with his drink he had the fire going and was just lighting a cigarette. 'You used not to smoke,' I said, handing him his glass.

'I used not to do a lot of things.' He inhaled deeply and tossed the lighter on to the coffee table. 'If you're going to stay sane when you're inside, you each develop your own survival-kit.' He glanced at me. 'You remember a lot, don't you? Too damned much. I'm not Roger Sutton. Not the man you knew – or thought you knew. You knew him with a child's perception. You didn't know him at all.'

'I'm not so sure of that,' I said seriously. 'A child's perception can be awfully clear, sometimes, because it isn't clouded by an adult's sometimes false values and expectations.'

'Then you should leave your memories of me where they belong – in the past.'

'We've been over that.'

There was a little silence while I tried to think of the best way to ask him about his present family, without making him clam up. Before I could, he said casually, 'Where are you painting?'

'Out at the home of some people called Norris. It's off on a side road from –'

'Yes, I know it. Plumbers get to know places.' He took a swallow from the whisky. 'Nice for you to have friends in the area. Have you known them long?'

I shook my head. 'I didn't know them at all. I was

looking for places to paint and the estate agent mentioned their place, so I went and asked if they'd mind if I painted the scene looking down the valley. They've been very nice about it.'

Even though they don't really like me being there, I reflected silently. Well, hard luck, folks, because you're stuck with me till I satisfy myself that Vi's fears for her life were groundless and a figment of hysterical imagination. I'm the substitute for Lillian Ballard, though you don't know it – the understudy suddenly pushed into the starring role before she's learned all her lines.

'Will you show me some of your paintings?' Roger was asking. 'No, I guess that's silly. You'd hardly carry them with you.'

'Well, no. Only the one I'm working on, and it's a bit early to say how that will work out.'

I produced the partly-finished article and he looked at it for a long time in silence. 'Do you sell much stuff?' he asked eventually.

'A few. Not as many as I'd like, and not for as much as I'd like, either.' I smiled.

'My guess would be that it'll happen.' He glanced at his watch. 'Good night,' he said briefly, and went.

I felt disappointment wash over me that he had cut the visit so short, but at least we had held the nearest thing to a normal conversation. He had shown genuine interest in my painting, which was getting close to showing interest in his daughter as a person. I· picked up his empty glass and noticed he had left his cigarette-lighter – a handsome silver one. I picked it up. It was engraved: *Roger from Sally, but I wish you'd stop smoking*. I smiled. Sally most probably was his wife, and something about the inscription suggested a warm kind of relationship. Roger would be back some time for that lighter.

As I turned to take the glass out to the kitchen, a movement at the window caught my eye. Though it was gone in a flash, there was no mistake: it had been a face – a woman's face had been peering through the window at me.

Without even stopping to think I raced outside.

By the house-light spilling through the front door I saw a figure slipping through the partial cover of the trees towards the garden gate. She heard me, of course, and began to run, but I had the advantage of being already at full running speed and driven by a flare of anger at having someone snooping around. Anger prevented me from realizing that rushing out alone to apprehend the snooper might not be healthy. The woman fumbled at the gate-latch.

'Stop!' I ordered, and grabbed her arm.

She stopped at once and turned to face me. No one I had ever seen before.

'What do you want?' I demanded. 'What are you doing here?'

She was breathing hard, from distress, not exertion, I guessed. The light from the front door fell full on her and I saw a woman of perhaps forty-one or two, of medium height, good figure in slacks and sweater; but because I had my back to the light she wouldn't have been able to see my features at all, though she was staring at me with a kind of desperate intensity.

'Who are you?' she said sharply, almost as if our roles were reversed, and I was the intruder.

'I might,' I answered curtly, 'ask you the same question.'

'I'm Roger Miller's wife. I'm Sally Miller.'

Perhaps it shouldn't have been so unexpected, but I released her arm and stepped back as if I'd been hit.

There were a couple of silent seconds. 'I see,' I said slowly. 'We need to talk, then. Will you come in?'

She followed me silently into the house. 'Sit by the fire,' I said quietly. 'You're cold.' She was shivering slightly, though I suspected it was as much with distress as the chilly night air. 'I'll get you a drink.'

I could use one myself, I reflected as I went out to the kitchen. When I came back Sally Miller was staring at the fire. As I handed her the glass she looked up at me with appraising, troubled eyes. 'Thank you.' She sipped the drink and watched me as I put some more wood on the fire and sat down in the chair opposite hers.

'I had no right to spy on you like that,' she said. 'I suppose it seems an unpardonable thing to do.'

'A pretty human sort of thing to do, though,' I said. 'You knew your husband had been seeing me, I gather – though it's only been a very few times.'

'I knew he'd been seeing someone – or, more correctly, I knew something had happened to him, something that greatly disturbed him. And obviously he was going to see someone tonight and his explanation of where he was going didn't ring true, so I followed him.'

She looked squarely at me. 'That's no excuse for spying on you, perhaps. But I'm not just playing the jealous wife. There's more to it than that sort of situation, isn't there?'

I hesitated, and Sally Miller, staring at me, said softly, 'Oh, my God. You're his daughter, aren't you?'

Exactly what made her so certain, I couldn't be sure – a resemblance she saw, intuition – but she was certain, and there seemed to me no point in trying to deny it, as presumably Roger would have insisted I should.

'Yes,' I said quietly. She went on staring at me in a kind of bewilderment. 'Look,' I said, 'I'm sorry you've been worried about this. I certainly never wanted –'

'But *why?*' Sally cut in, not even hearing me. 'Why has he never talked of you? Why is he afraid of you?'

'Afraid?'

'Oh, yes. That's why I had to find out who it was he was coming to see. How long have you been here?'

'About ten days.' It seemed a year, at times.

She nodded. 'Ever since you came, he's been different. Silent; then too talkative and falsely bright, as if to convince everyone there's nothing wrong. When I tried to talk about it he said I was imagining it. But I wasn't. But – what is so terrible about having a daughter, that he should want to hide it? Does he think I imagine there wasn't ever another woman in his life? Does he think I would care? Why wouldn't he talk about you?'

'I think,' I said carefully, 'he might have been very bitter over the divorce. My mother and him. He dropped out of our lives a long time ago – even changed his name. It's taken me an age to find him. I guess I bring all the old unhappy memories back.'

Sally Miller was still white-faced and unconvinced. 'He has nightmares now,' she said slowly. 'He never did before. Not like this, anyway. He cries out in his sleep. Usually it's just sounds – disjointed – not words I can distinguish. But last night he said: "He's dead. My God, he's dead!" It was – a cry of horror. Why? What did he mean?'

I felt painfully sorry for this woman with the intelligent face who, I felt, must learn the crushing truth my father had tried to hide from her. Yet I felt suddenly that Sally Miller would not be crushed by it. Anguished, battered, but not crushed into defeat. But the truth must come from Roger, not from me.

I dodged the question. 'There's no accounting for what we think in nightmares.'

'But his nightmare doesn't go away, even when he's awake. What did he mean?' She was concentrated; intense, hazel eyes searching mine. 'You know, don't you?'

'I haven't seen him since I was six years old,' I said. 'My mother has never talked about him.'

Sally was not to be put off. 'Did he – please, you must tell me –'

'Tell you what?' Roger snapped from the doorway, and I remembered with a leaden feeling in my stomach that I hadn't locked the front door.

'You left your lighter,' I said in a senseless effort to reduce the scene to something like normality.

'I came back for it.' He hadn't taken his eyes off his wife. 'I found more than I bargained for.'

He was clearly in a black rage, and with a painful twist somewhere inside me I saw that it was the desperate rage of a cornered animal fighting for its life.

'What the hell are you doing here, Sally? What's going on? What must Lyn tell you?'

She faced his transparent fury coolly, almost as if unaware of it. 'I have to know,' she said. 'Did you kill someone?'

He whirled on me. 'What have you been telling her?' His voice was almost a snarl.

'She hasn't been telling me anything,' Sally said steadily, and I understood then that their relationship was such that she was not afraid of his anger turning into physical violence, and she never would be.

She went on, 'I came here to find out who it was you were seeing, who it was who had frightened you so much. And don't deny you've been frightened: frightened to the point of having nightmares when you cried out that someone was dead. I have to know. For my sake. For your sake. I can't help you if I don't know.'

He stared at her. 'You want to help me?'

'Of course.'

'Then forget it. Forget you ever saw Lyn. Leave it where it belongs – buried in the past.'

'I can't. You must realize that. You must. Whatever it is, *you* can't leave it buried. None of us can walk away from the past and imagine it doesn't exist. Whatever has happened has happened, and all eternity can't alter it. I've always known, of course, that there was something, because of the great gap of years you wouldn't ever talk about. You must realize that. I accepted you for what you are and I told myself I didn't care about those missing years. But that's no longer true. I suppose it never was true.'

He turned on me again. 'You bloody little *fool!* Now do you understand what you've done? I told you to stay out of my life. But you knew better, didn't you? You had to go on meddling. You had to destroy everything!'

'Stop it!' Sally said sharply. 'She's your daughter. She hasn't destroyed anything. I told you: I accepted you – blank years and all the threat they carried – for what you are. No one can change the past, but it's what we build on it that matters. But now I have to know about the blank years. Whatever they hide. They don't change anything, Roger. Whether or not I know what you did, doesn't change what you are. Did you kill someone?'

Roger was still staring at me. More correctly, he was looking straight through me as if I didn't exist, and only he could know what he was seeing. For perhaps a full thirty seconds he didn't move, and Sally must have known the answer before he turned to look at her.

'I did twelve years for killing a night-watchman in the course of a robbery,' he said flatly. 'Those are the years I haven't talked about.'

Sally just went on looking at him silently. Perhaps she had expected something like that for a long time.

'Did you kill him?' I asked softly.

He gave a short, contemptuous laugh, and said to Sally, 'Because I pleaded not guilty to the murder charge in court, Lyn still cherishes some romantic notion I might be exonerated some day. What fool is going to plead guilty to a murder charge if there's even the faintest chance he might get off? Pleading not guilty in court doesn't mean anything.'

'You're not in court now,' Sally said.

'Look,' he said more quietly, 'I suppose I can understand that you both want me to say I didn't kill that night-watchman. I've already explained to Lyn: I pleaded guilty to the break-and-enter charge because they had me cold on that. I was a panicky amateur and I left a tool behind – a drill with my name on it. It was like a come-up-and-see-me-sometime note. I also had in my possession an emerald pendant – easily identified. I told you I was an amateur: having got the damned thing I didn't know how to get rid of it for good folding cash. I told the jury that was the only piece I got: someone beat me to the job, and that someone killed the security-patrol man and missed that pendant. I've never changed that story. I'm not changing it now. I like it. It's grown on me. The jury didn't believe me because they had more sense than to swallow such a silly story. You say you just want the truth. Funny, isn't it? If I say I killed that man, you'll believe me. If I say I didn't, you'll still never know if it's the truth or not. That's what you *want* me to say, but you won't know if you can believe it.'

He spread his hands. 'So that is the bright, glorious wonderful truth you've both been so anxious to uncover. So where do we go from here?'

Sally stood up. 'Home,' she said simply. 'We have to tell Brent and Rosemary.'

'Never!' All the fury was back on the surface again. 'Are you mad?'

Then suddenly he went very still, and I saw the anger replaced by the fear that had fuelled it.

'I've lost you all, haven't I?' he said dully.

'Of course not.' Sally took his arm. 'I told you: it's what you are now that matters. You're still the same man I loved a fortnight ago, before any of this started. It'll be all right. There might be some rough patches, but we'll be all right. But we have to tell the children.'

'Why? Why do they have to know?'

'Because one day they're sure to find out. They'll begin wondering about the years you never talk about, and they'll begin checking. If your daughter could find you now, your step-children can find your past. It would be much worse for them if it happened like that.'

'Oh, God,' was all he said.

Sally looked at me. Heaven knows what she was really feeling. 'Thank you, Lyn. May I come to see you again?'

'Of course,' I said. My father didn't look at me as they went out.

I shut the door, pulled the curtains and sat by the fire. It was hours later I remembered I hadn't eaten anything. I had a sandwich, and a sleepless night.

Five

I was in no mental state to do any painting the next day. Almost automatically I drove out towards the Norris house, more because I needed something to do than for any other reason. Before I got to their turn-off I remembered Arnold Bright had spoken of Mt Bartholomew as being the place where Peter had injured his spine – about a twenty-minute drive, he had said. I stopped the car and pulled out my road-map. If I couldn't concentrate on painting, I had better find something else to take my mind off last night.

There was a side road which was marked on the map 'unsealed' and ended in nothing, but bore the name Mt Bartholomew Road, so I went along till I found the turn-off, though it wasn't signposted. Although passable, it was clearly little used and simply wound its way among trees and ended in a clearing which evidently had once been a house-site, but the house was long gone and the cleared area was gradually being reclaimed by the bush. There was still a timber shed standing, looking in quite good repair.

A couple of hundred metres to the south was the edge of the escarpment – the south face where Vi and Arnold had planned to climb down to the cave entrance, I guessed; the south face where, Arnold said, whoever was using that damaged rope would have been killed. Vi's rope. Vi's climb. I walked down to the edge and looked over, and was instantly swamped by my unreasoning fear of anything higher than a six-foot step-ladder.

There was an almost sheer drop of perhaps three

hundred metres to a thickly timbered valley. I retreated several paces, my feet and hands prickling with the almost unbearable sensation only those who suffer that terrible height-induced panic can understand. I dropped to my hands and knees and crawled back towards the edge, then lay flat on my stomach to peer over, doggedly telling myself over and over not to be such a fool – I couldn't possibly fall. I failed to properly convince myself.

There were sheer walls with only precarious hand-and-foot holds, where dependence on a rope would be vital. It was not, I knew, a cliff which would present anything more than an interesting challenge to experienced rock-climbers and abseilers – that unfathomable breed, as far as I was concerned, who respect heights but have no fear of them, and indeed are stimulated by them. I have no more comprehension of their apparently nonchalant skill than they would have of my blind fear. I couldn't see where the entrance to the cave was, and obviously Vi or Arnold must have seen it from either the valley below or the mountain opposite.

I retreated from the cliff edge. The south face I had just left was at the head of the short, timbered valley. A fairly narrow ridge ran off at an angle to continue the chain of mountains, and the other side of the ridge, I gathered, must be the east face, where Peter had fallen. I walked across, perhaps four hundred metres, reflecting that if the caves were linked it must be a fairly extensive system and so presumably would be quite exciting, if your idea of recreation was to slide and scramble down a cliff with, at times, only a few strands of rope between you and disaster, and then follow that up by crawling and clambering with torches and helmet-lamps in pitch darkness over confusing, boulder-filled tunnels in the ground. I'd prefer tennis.

I sat for a while at a safe distance from the edge and looked at the blunt, forested mountains and thought of the Norris household and tried desperately to keep my thoughts away from Roger and Sally and Sally's children. They had filled my sleepless night hours.

The warmth of the autumn sun crept into me in a tranquillizing inertia, when although my brain kept churning over events and old thoughts, my body sat still. Eventually I became aware of the activity all around me. In my stillness I had become just part of the scenery as far as the wildlife was concerned, and I understood why Peter had been content, originally, to just be here with his camera while Vi and Arnold went caving. Even at this time of year, with winter approaching, there was an abundance of bird-life, unafraid of me because they rarely saw humans. A couple of kangaroos grazed lazily, and a mouse – or something that looked like a mouse to me – scuttled busily about, not two metres from me.

But even the delight in watching them was presently wiped from my mind by wondering how Sally's children had reacted to learning about their step-father's past; by hearing Vi's voice, tense and anxious, saying: 'She's dangerous.'

Dangerous. I looked around and got to my feet. I wasn't entirely sure why I had come here. Perhaps a feeling I needed to see the place where, I presumed, Vi's fears for her life had begun. Though why she would feel the damaged rope was anything more than an accident, I couldn't imagine, unless something else had happened, something I didn't know about. Or unless it was all due to some kind of paranoia which only affected her at times.

I sighed and walked restlessly over to the shed. Apparently it had been some kind of storage shed or barn when the farm had been operative. It had a couple of tiny windows about a foot square and a door which opened outward and fastened on the outside with a bar across it which slotted into brackets. The place was in good repair, and a glance through a window showed a couple of wooden packing cases, a bench and some old hessian sacks, everything dusty and unused.

It was depressingly in keeping with my mood. It reminded me that an active Peter who could run and jump had no doubt used the shed as a hide while he aimed his camera and his life's ambitions at the small wild creatures which came confidently around, believing they were unobserved. And long before Peter, there had been a house here – some sort of small farm, probably. Someone had set up a home here, had brought their hopes and dreams. And had failed.

Failed just as miserably as I had failed. I had come here full of hope that I would get to know my father and be able to form my own judgment of him – and, if I was to be entirely honest, I had cherished the hope that at worst he would tell me the exact circumstances that had made him kill the patrolman; or, at best, tell me convincingly that he had not killed him at all. And I had not achieved any of these things, and quite probably I had destroyed his present family life as well, just as he had said I would. I had been too concerned with my own feelings to believe him. It was no comfort to me now that Sally had pointed out, as I had, that they very likely would have learned the truth some day even if I had never come here.

And for a while I had thought I might be of some help to a terrified woman, might even – wonderful me – be the means of saving her life. The only problem with *that* was that she had no intention of confiding in me and apparently no recollection of making a frantic plea for help. Unless that cryptic 'She's dangerous' remark had some significance. *Ivan would laugh and make a joke of it.* Ivan, it seemed, was on the right track.

In any case, my painting would soon be finished, and my excuse for being at the Norris house would have run out, unless I simply painted something else there. I walked back to my car, wishing bitterly that I had never come here.

I drove back to the cottage and spent the rest of the day in dogged physical activity to try to put my thoughts away for a while, and make myself tired enough to be sure of sleeping. I raked leaves in the garden, mowed grass which had grown no more than a centimetre, washed windows, then walked for a couple of hours, briskly and aimlessly, around the town. By the time it was dusk I felt I was exhausted enough to sleep the clock around. I showered, pulled on jeans and a sweater, and sat in front of the fire with a book belonging to Lillian Ballard.

I was just beginning to think of getting a meal when the doorbell rang. Liam Stuart, impeccable in grey suit, smiled at me. 'Hello. Sorry if I'm a bit early. There's no rush.'

I blinked. It took me probably three full seconds to remember he'd asked me to dinner. I was glad I was standing with my back to the light so he couldn't see the expression on my face.

'Yes. I mean, no, I don't think you're early. I'm – awfully late. I shan't be more than ten minutes. Will you pour yourself a drink? Sit by the fire.'

With that I left him to think what he chose and when I returned in fractionally under the promised ten minutes, wearing a dark green woollen suit and what I hoped was an unflurried air, he was on his feet in a moment with no hint that I hadn't carried it off to perfection.

It was only much later after a leisurely meal, during which he had proved very pleasant company, that Liam looked at me searchingly and said quietly, 'Lyn, is anything wrong?'

'Wrong?' I echoed brightly. 'No, of course not. The meal's delicious.'

'I wasn't thinking about the food.'

I met his steady eyes, and smiled ruefully. 'I didn't sleep last night. Just one of those things. I'm sorry if it shows.'

'As long as that's all. Do you work on your paintings at night sometimes, or do you have to have the scene there in front of you all the time?'

'I often work without the scene being physically there, as long as it's in my mind.'

I didn't tell him that I was spending a greatly exaggerated amount of time on-the-spot at the moment because I'd been flung into the detective business. I realized he'd steered the conversation to focus on me all evening, and had offered very little information about himself, even when I'd tried to glean some.

'You said you were on holiday here, too,' I commented. 'What is your work?'

'Oh, I have a public service job. Pretty ordinary sort of stuff. Overseeing government regulations, that sort of thing. I'm on extended leave at the moment to recover from getting myself knocked about a bit. I'm trying to get the body used to some activity again.'

'A motor accident?' I asked.

He smiled. 'Well, my mother always told me motorcycles were dangerous.'

'And now you're riding one again?'

'Oh, that. Well, isn't that something to do with psychology? You get back on the horse that threw you. Otherwise you lose your nerve.'

'How badly were you hurt?'

'No bones broken. What goes under the heading of internal injuries. I'm mending very well.' He said the last sentence as though he were trying to convince himself.

He looked down at the wine in his glass for a moment and then looked at me. 'What family do you have, to worry whether you're starving in a garret while you wait for your paintings to be recognized?'

'My parents separated when I was a little girl. I lived with my mother, and a later-acquired stepfather, till I was old enough to go it alone. No brothers or sisters.'

'Keep in touch with your father?'

'Very occasionally,' I said.

He nodded, and to my relief began talking about one of the books he'd seen at Lillian's while he was waiting for me to change.

Later in the evening as I slid thankfully into bed and let exhaustion plunge me down toward sleep, I reflected that Liam Stuart was a very pleasant man, well-read and intelligent, and beyond that I had learned nothing of him at all.

The days ran on and became weeks, as days have a disconcerting habit of doing, and seeing Liam Stuart became a habit also. I explored the district for subjects to paint. More than once Liam came with me, surprising me with his knowledge of the locality; several times he took me to dinner. But he remained strangely unknown. For me he was almost a man without a past, without a background, but since he was a delightful companion who seemed content to remain just a totally undemanding friend, I made no real effort to enquire into his life. But I realized uneasily that whatever his feelings were, he was beginning to reach a disturbing degree of importance to me.

I worked on several paintings, partly because I wanted deliberately to stretch out the time I had as an excuse for visiting the Norris house so that I would be available for Vi to appeal to for help, though with time passing I became more sure the panic that had swept her had been the product of some sort of nervous disorder.

Of the Millers I saw nothing, and felt it best to stay out of their lives for a while.

On one particular day, as I had been out to dinner with Liam the night before, I slept late and it was past lunch-time when I drove out to the Norris house. Two or three more days, I decided, and I would quit this charade. Whatever occasional hallucinations Vi Norris suffered from, clearly there was nothing I could do.

Peter was just coming in his wheelchair down the path from the Fairy Wood. He had a camera with a good-looking zoom lens on his lap, and a tripod tucked behind him against the back of the chair.

'Hello,' I said as I got out of the car. I nodded at the camera. 'Get anything?'

'Nothing special. You have to do a lot of waiting to get anything special. Or you have to be lucky.'

'I can believe it. I went out to Mt Bartholomew one day,' I told him, and saw his face go carefully blank. 'There must have been a house there once.'

'Some people called Bartholomew lived there ages ago. That's how it got its name.'

'Arnold Bright told me you found it a good place for photography, and I found out why. I sat still for a while and all manner of birds and things came quite close.'

He nodded. 'Bartholomews planted trees and shrubs that birds like, and now there's no one there to disturb them. There's a shed there that still makes a good hide, now that I'm in this.' He tapped the chair.

'You still go there?'

'Arnold has taken me a couple of times.' He bent his head, fiddling with the camera.

'I'll take you any time you want to go,' I said.

He looked up quickly, appraisingly. 'Would you?' He sounded more cautious than enthusiastic. 'It can be pretty boring to most people.'

'I'd like to do it. Would you show me some of your photographs?'

Again the doubtful look. 'If you like,' he said politely. I walked beside his chair to the house and waved to Vi, who was just settling herself down with a book in her favourite spot in the little courtyard.

Arnold Bright had been right. Peter's photographs were good. They were very good indeed. It was a little hard to realize that they were the work of someone who was scarcely more than a child. They were not merely identification-type photographs of the local birds and animals – they had a distinctive quality of real artistry about them: a honey-eater at sunrise amid a spangle of dewdrops, a willy-wagtail in full scolding flutter above the head of an impassive kookaburra, a single kangaroo a silhouette against a mist-filled valley.

Encouraged by my interest, Peter became relaxed and enthusiastic, and we could discuss various aspects of his work – things like the use of perspective for certain effects, or how to focus the eye of the beholder in a special area – on a common footing, and for a while I think we both forgot that he could no longer scramble through the bush in pursuit of his beloved wild creatures with no aim to capture anything but their image on film.

As he ruffled through a desk drawer for a photograph he wanted to show me, he picked up one of himself, bare-headed, wind-tousled, in boots and jeans and sweater carrying his own camera and laughing at the photographer who snapped his picture. He handed it to me rather quickly. 'You can have it if you like,' he said. I was greatly touched.

We had been poring over the photographs for some time

when the sound of a car outside made Peter glance out of the widow. 'Oh-oh,' he said. 'Arnold's here to help me with my science stuff and I haven't had lunch. Waylay him and lavish your charms on him while I belt out to the kitchen for a sandwich, will you?'

He looked at me with such a normal mischievous boy's grin that my heart gave a lurch. This was Peter as I hadn't seen him. Not the haunted, tight-faced crippled boy, but the zestful teenager he should have been.

'How much charm do I have to lay on?' I asked.

'Enough for me to scoff two peanut-butter sandwiches. I'm starving.'

'Two sandwiches' worth of waylaying coming up,' I promised, and he laughed and wheeled off toward the kitchen.

I stumbled outside, blinded by sudden unexpected tears, and almost literally bumped into Arnold Bright.

'What's wrong?' he asked anxiously.

I shook my head and swallowed. 'Peter laughed,' I said stupidly. 'He was showing me his photographs,' I added, as if that explained everything. Perhaps it did.

'Oh, I see.' Arnold nodded. 'Yes. I know. It makes you feel like that.' He touched my arm. 'Peter will adjust. He'll turn his talents in some other direction that he *can* achieve from a wheelchair. I knew Peter before this happened. He's shattered, now; quite changed from what he used to be. But given time he'll pick himself up, because he's not a quitter. I'm sure having you around is good for him.'

'I'll have finished my painting, soon. There won't be any reason for me to come here.'

'If you can spare the time to drop in occasionally I really think it would help Peter.'

I looked at him for a moment, wanting to tell him that it was Vi I had come here to help, only to find she didn't seem to want or need help. But I didn't tell him. I didn't know him enough to trust him with that kind of a confidence. I didn't know anything about anyone, I thought frustratedly.

'Peter was up at the Fairy Wood with his camera, so he's

running late for his science lesson because he's just gone out to the kitchen for a sandwich,' I said. 'I've been detailed to waylay you.'

He chuckled. 'Right. There's a book in the library I want to check out, anyway, so I'll do that while I'm waiting. I'm sure you're anxious to get on with your painting, so consider me waylaid as instructed.' He smiled at me and added with swift seriousness, 'Try to give Peter some of your time, Lyn. If he showed you his photographs he regards you as his friend. And he has so few.'

He went off and I walked out to my car to get my painting gear, wondering if it was worthwhile setting it up this late in the day. Edith Wishart's car was parked outside the door to her granny-flat. Evidently she'd been shopping, because she came out to the car and took a couple of supermarket-type bags of groceries out of the boot. We waved to each other and I went around to my painting-spot in front of the house to assess the light in the valley. It was still good enough to justify maybe an hour's work, I decided. The sun was still warm enough for Vi to be enjoying her favourite spot in the courtyard, engrossed in her book, with her little radio playing beside her, looking a picture of untroubled relaxation.

And then I saw death rolling down the hill towards her.

Edith Wishart's Peugeot, parked up the hill and on the sloping ramp that led to her door had begun to run down the slope. The total distance was less than fifty metres, but the slope was steep enough for the car to pick up speed alarmingly. Vi, intent on her book, the radio covering the sound of tyres softly crunching on gravel and grass, had her back turned, totally oblivious. And she was squarely in its path.

'Vi!' I shouted. 'Run!'

Her head came up enquiringly as I ran towards her. In the race to reach her first, I had less distance to cover than the car, but the car was travelling much faster. In the five or six seconds before impact, I saw everything with as much clarity of detail as if I could watch it all on a slow-motion film.

There was no one behind the wheel of the Peugeot. The combination of hill-slope and ramp-angle were sufficient to launch it directly at Vi's chair. I saw her lower her book and look at me, puzzled, keeping her place in the book carefully with one thumb.

'Behind you! Run!' I was shouting. She began to stand up, her expression changing to alarm but not comprehension, as I cannoned into her in some kind of imitation of the flying tackle a rugby player might use to try to force an opponent out over the touch-line.

I felt a bruising impact on my left thigh and then Vi and I fell together in an undignified heap while beside us there was a crushing sound of splintering furniture and glass and grinding metal.

There was a second of stunned stillness, filled with the smell of dust. Then I scrambled to my feet.

'Vi! Are you all right?'

She was sitting up, staring from me to the car that was standing where it had finished up against the wall of the house, amongst the wreckage of patio furniture, smashed bricks and crushed garden shrubs.

I heard Arnold Bright shout, 'What was that?' from inside the house.

Vi stood up. 'Oh, my God,' she said faintly.

I grabbed her arm, shaking her. 'Who's trying to kill you?' I demanded. 'Tell me!'

She seemed too shocked to understand what I had said and just shook her head. Then there were running footsteps and Ivan and Arnold arrived from different directions with anxious questions.

Vi seemed to suddenly realize what had happened. 'I was sitting there!' she said, pointing at the damaged wall of the house. The now-silent radio lay under the car, and the book had been flung out on to the lawn.

'Lucky you saw the car in time,' Ivan said.

'I didn't. Lyn grabbed me. The radio was playing. I didn't hear anything and I had my back turned, so I didn't see it. If Lyn hadn't –' She broke off and Ivan put his arms around her.

'Don't think of it. You're all right. Nothing happened to you except a fright. Just hang on to that thought.' He looked across at me. 'It took a lot of guts to do what you did. You couldn't have had much time.'

I shook my head. 'It was just an instinctive reaction. There wasn't time to get scared.'

I looked up to where the car had come from. Peter had come out on to the concrete garden path that led down to the house from Mrs Wishart's cottage; Edith Wishart was standing at her front door. Both were staring down at us.

Vi turned to me. 'You saved my life, Lyn.'

I smiled shakily. 'Well, that's something we can't ever know. Probably saved you some injuries, but they mightn't even have been serious. And as I said, it wasn't anything heroic – it was pure reflex.'

I saw Peter spin his chair around and wheel back swiftly into the house, but not before I was struck by the expression on his face. All trace of the animation that had been there a few minutes before when he had shown me his photographs, was gone – replaced by the pale bitter stoniness. It must have brought all the memories of his own accident pouring back.

Edith Wishart came running down the path, surprisingly agile for her years but not, I suspected, entirely sober, though shock had probably had a sobering influence.

'Is anyone hurt? Where's Peter?' There was anguished anxiety in her voice and in her face.

'No one's hurt, Aunt Edith,' Ivan reassured her. 'It was pretty close, and but for Lyn, Vi certainly would have been hurt.'

'Thank God,' Mrs Wishart said faintly. 'But – the car. I don't understand.'

'I'm afraid it must have been parked in neutral,' Arnold Bright suggested. 'Maybe you forgot to pull the handbrake on.'

'I wouldn't park it in neutral,' she said firmly.

'Well, let's check,' Ivan said. He opened the passenger-side front door of the car and leaned in. 'Mmm. Well, there's the answer, I'm afraid. Gear-lever's in neutral and the handbrake's only pulled on a notch or two – and that hand-brake needs attention anyway. I've heard you complain it's become faulty.'

'I don't believe it.' She went to the car herself and checked, then stepped back and straightened up slowly, suddenly looking old. She shook her head. 'I can't think how I could have done that. I never park in neutral.'

'Maybe not when you're sober,' Vi said curtly.

Edith Wishart just stood staring at the car and the wreckage of furniture. 'I'm most terribly sorry,' she said presently. 'I'll pay for the damage, of course.'

'Oh, insurance will take care of the bit of damage to the wall and the furniture. It's nothing much. Not even much to the car, I think,' Ivan said. 'It might be driveable. I'll try.'

It was not driveable, with radiator and fan jammed together as well as a crumpled mudguard and smashed headlight. Ivan took Vi's arm. 'Better come in and rest a bit. A stiff drink might be in order. I'll get hold of the insurance people and so forth, Aunt Edith. Lyn, you might go up with Aunt Edith and see she has a cup of *tea*.' He put emphasis on the last word with a faint lift of one eyebrow at me. 'And see you have something yourself. And thank you.'

When I began to walk I was forced sharply to recall that my left leg had received a glancing blow from either the car or a bit of flying debris, and I winced at the soreness. Arnold noticed.

'You're hurt,' he said.

I shook my head. 'Only a bit of a bruise.'

'I'm most terribly sorry,' Edith said again as I walked with her to her flat. 'I can't think how I could have done such a stupid thing. You might have been killed. Or Vi. And if Peter had been in the way –'

'Well, no one was really hurt. Try not to worry about it. We all make mistakes sometimes.'

She was obviously very distressed and I made her sit down while I put the electric kettle on to boil. I stood at the door for a moment, looking at the path the car had taken, and I felt cold as I pictured Vi sitting there, her back turned, the radio playing to cover any sound of rolling wheels. Right in the path of the parked car. Had Aunt Edith forgotten to put the car in gear and pull the hand-brake on?

Or had someone seen an opportunity to stage another accident? It would take only seconds to slip the gear into neutral and release the brake. The car would have needed only the gentlest push to launch it on its way. Who had the opportunity? The answer was simple: anyone. Edith Wishart, obviously. And once she had gone into her flat, anyone else with enough nerve could have done it. Ivan was somewhere about, because he'd been on the scene in seconds. Arnold Bright had *said* he was going into the library, but he'd have no witnesses. Peter? Hardly Peter. And any person unknown who happened to be lurking with murderous intent could have come and gone unseen under cover of the garden shrubs and trees, just as it would have been possible to destroy Vi's climbing ropes and leave an apparently accidentally-overturned old car battery to take the blame.

But, in the end, sheer accident was by far the most likely: Edith coming home a bit tizzy and failing to park properly. I had seen her taking groceries out of the boot. The simple action of slamming the boot-lid closed could easily have been enough to set the car in motion – so slowly inching forward at first that she would never have noticed it as she turned away to go back indoors. But by the time I had walked around to the front of the house and back again the car was in full flight. A simple, straightforward accident.

I went back into the kitchen and made coffee for us both. Edith Wishart was sitting in the living-room that opened off the kitchen, staring at nothing. She took the steaming mug from me without a word and I sat in a chair opposite hers.

'You told me,' I said quietly, 'that you never drove when you've been drinking.'

She shook her head. 'I never do. Only today –'

She stopped, and I prompted, 'Today? What was different today?'

She gave an odd little laugh. 'Do you ever get the feeling something is *wrong* and you can't put your finger on it?'

'Yes,' I said softly, willing her to go on.

'Well, don't *try* to put your finger on it. You might get burnt.'

And she laughed again and said, 'Perhaps I should give up driving the car. Your leg got hurt. Is it just a bruise? I'll give you some ice to put on it.'

Quite clearly she was not going to tell me what she had almost put her finger on.

As I was leaving, the westerly-sliding sun hanging low above the ridge where the Norris road ran back to the main road, something across on the ridge among the trees caught my eye: a quick glint of sunlight striking on glass or metal. Something moving, above the road, where nothing using glass or metal should be moving.

I slid into the car and reached into the glove-box for the binoculars I habitually carried there for catching a closer glimpse of a bird, or deciding whether a distant bend in a river, or a far farmhouse was worth a closer look as a possible subject for a painting.

From the shelter of the car I trained the binoculars on the area where I had seen that quick reflected glint. It took me several seconds to find him. He was sitting among some bracken ferns, elbows on knees, watching this house with binoculars of his own, too far away for me to be able to identify him, even if he was someone I knew.

In something much nearer anger than fear, I picked out a big old tree to serve as a landmark, put the binoculars away and started the car. I wanted to see just who was spying on the Norris household. I drove rather faster than usual, the tyres sending up little splatters of gravel against the underside of the car as I took the corner. Still too angry to wonder if I was running into danger, I stopped the car abreast of my landmark tree and scrambled up the embankment.

It was easy enough to find the spot where he had been sitting. The ferns were flattened down to indicate that; but whoever the observer was, he had gone and a careful search showed he had not been obliging enough to leave any clues to his identity – no cigarette butts, no discarded wrapper off a chocolate bar, for what any of that would have been worth.

I had a sudden thought that he might not have gone very far. Suppose he had simply withdrawn into cover of the trees at my approach and was watching me? It would be perfectly clear that I had seen him, and he might not be at all kindly disposed towards me. My courage evaporated in a flash and getting back to the car seemed a particularly good idea.

As I pushed back through the ferns and other light undergrowth of the forest I found the watcher had left a clue after all. Behind a bush at the edge of the road there were fresh tyre-marks in a patch of bare earth still damp from an early-morning shower.

A single set of tracks. A motorcycle had been parked there.

Obviously he of the binoculars had left, so, as he was not lurking in the undergrowth with murderous thoughts about me, I got a pad and pencil from the car and made a sketch of the tyre-marks. If I saw a motorcycle with tyres whose tread made that pattern I had a suspect at least, even though there were doubtless many motorcycles with similar tyres, and this set were not obliging enough to have some kind of distinctive fault or damage to make them readily identifiable. And of course, the watcher with the binoculars could easily have been an innocent bird-watcher following the flight of a rufous whistler or something.

I sighed and ran my fingers wearily through my hair. All reasoning aside, I really had no doubt who had been here. Ever since I had come to this place, a motorcycle had seemed to haunt me. *Why?*

And why did I feel this behaviour was so at odds with the nature of the man who had taken me to dinner last night?

Subterfuge, spying – it seemed totally out of character in the man who, in the weeks I had known him, had been courteous, considerate, and a delightful companion.

My bruised leg was aching. I slid into the car and drove home.

Six

I had a long, hot bath, and by the time I had dressed again I had made a decision. Two, actually.

The first, which I had always more or less known, was that I was a coward. The second, which was really part of the first, was that tomorrow I would pack my bags and go. Coming here had been a disaster.

My father didn't want to know me and had accused me of wrecking his efforts to rebuild his life; and he was very probably right. I had become too much involved in the problems of Vi Norris and I was achieving precisely nothing there, either. And I was caught up in some vague and uncertain involvement with a personable motorcyclist who, I felt, was more than he appeared on the surface.

And I had had enough of them all. I'd given Vi ample opportunity to confide in me if she was as terrified as her anguished note to Lillian indicated. She had chosen not to trust me. If she got herself killed there was nothing I could do about it.

On that firm decision I went to bed early and, surprisingly, slept quickly and heavily.

Shortly after I woke next morning the phone rang and Sally's voice asked anxiously, 'Lyn, will you come around this evening for dinner? There are things we all need to talk about.'

I hesitated. 'I'm sorry,' I said. 'I'm leaving this morning. Going home.'

'Leaving!' She sounded bewildered.

'I should never have come. Roger was right. I've done nothing but harm – to him, to you, to myself. I guess I was just plain selfish, thinking only of myself and what *I* wanted. And I was foolish enough to nurture some sort of immature dream that Roger might be glad to see me. I was wrong, all down the line. I've hurt you all by coming here, and if I stay I'm only going to compound that hurt. I'm terribly sorry for what I've done to you all. The only thing I can do now is get out and leave you alone.'

'No!' There was real urgency in her voice. 'You mustn't go. Please. I think you may be the only person who can help us all come to terms with the truth. You're a link with Roger's past – the only person we know who knew him before he went to jail. Don't go now. I want my children to meet you. You'll help them to get to know Roger.'

'I don't really see how,' I said. 'I don't know him myself.'

'You came here to find out what he's really like. You haven't given yourself – or him – much time. Please don't go. Not yet. And you mustn't blame yourself for what's happening to us. You will come tonight, won't you? About seven. Not just for the children and me. We're strangers and you don't owe us anything.'

'It isn't a matter of owing,' I began.

'Roger is your father,' Sally was saying. 'Maybe he's a stranger, too, and you don't owe him anything. But don't you owe *yourself* the chance to know him? Don't you – don't we all – owe the *truth* something?'

'Truth! How can we know what the truth is when he won't talk about it?' I said bitterly.

'Have you,' she asked quietly, 'asked yourself why he won't talk about it?'

'Of course I have. A hundred times a day. I can only conclude it's the same reason a serviceman who comes home from war won't talk about it – not *really* talk about it. Because it's too unutterably awful and he wants to shut it out. Because unless you were there, unless you were part of it, he believes you can't understand the awfulness. Maybe he thinks you shouldn't try.'

'Perhaps,' Sally said. Then she added after a moment, 'Sometimes I think it's something more than that with Roger. It's as though there's something else. Something not *finished* yet.'

Something not finished. I shivered without quite knowing why. The police hadn't recovered the gems. That was the thing that had always been there in my mind. Roger swore at his trial he didn't have them and never had – bar the one distinctive piece he'd had in his possession when they picked him up.

But was the jewellery still hidden somewhere, waiting for him to collect it? If that was so, then it was back in Queensland, surely; so why was he here? And why hadn't he collected it years ago? It was seven years since he'd been released: surely it would have been safe for him to try to market the stuff years ago.

'Lyn?' Sally's questioning voice came in my ear.

'Sorry. I was thinking. How much has Roger told you of the whole thing?'

'More or less what would have been in the newspapers, I should think – in condensed form. That he gained entry to the jewellery store through the roof, avoiding the alarm system, which he then shut down. That the safe was open and empty; the display shelves emptied of everything really valuable, just one emerald pendant dropped on the floor. That the night-watchman was found next morning dead in the lane at the back of the building, killed with a Stilson wrench which no one could prove or disprove was his, but which was the sort of thing a plumber would be sure to have several of.'

'Yes,' I said. 'That's about all I know. I read the newspaper accounts from library files, a few years ago. And the transcript of the trial.'

'But you don't believe that's the whole story?'

I frowned. 'I don't know. That's why I'm going. I don't know and I can't know the whole story because Roger won't tell the whole story.'

'Exactly. Do you see what you're saying? You don't believe it happened the way he claims, any more than the jury believed it, because it stretches coincidence too far to say that two people decided to burgle the same premises on the same night. That means –'

Her voice shook for a second, and then she took a quick breath and went on, 'That means either he was guilty as charged, or something very different happened which for some reason he won't talk about. And somehow that frightens me even more than if the prosecution got it right the first time.'

I found myself developing considerable respect for Roger's wife.

'It's far more likely,' I said, 'that he was guilty as charged. As for feeling it's not finished, I guess a crime never is really finished, is it? It goes on sending out waves like the proverbial stone thrown into a lake, and the ripples go on and on in all directions, washing over people. We all have to learn to live with it, somehow. You can't get the stone out of the lake again. Simply catching and punishing the criminal doesn't end the crime. I think that's why we're left with the "unfinished" feeling. I came here, I suppose, believing Roger was probably guilty, but wanting him to tell me exactly how it happened – why he committed the break-and-enter, exactly why he killed the watchman, whether he meant to kill him, whether he didn't care. I wanted to *know* him, that's all – wanted to know how he felt about it all now. But he won't let me get close enough.'

'Stay,' Sally urged. 'A little longer, anyway. Perhaps we can all get to know each other a little better, if you stay.'

I felt an intense sense of guilt. I had walked into the lives of four people and blown away the relationship they had. I couldn't see how staying on could do anything to mend that, but if Sally Miller believed it could, I owed her that much.

'I'll see you this evening,' I said.

It was going to be a strange dinner-party, I thought as I hung up.

Very well, I decided almost angrily. If I wasn't going to be allowed to back out of this situation, then I'd try confronting Vi once more to see if I could get some sort of reaction from her. If she believed – with or without reason – that her life was in danger, then yesterday's incident should have sharply heightened her fears. With or without reason. She might now be so desperately in need of a friend that I would do to fill the vacancy left by Lillian Ballard.

As I got into the car and backed it down the driveway, I tried again to decide whether I thought it might have been an attempt on her life. First, how efficient was it? Not very — rather hit-and-miss. As it turned out, it probably would have been fatal, bearing in mind the smashed furniture, the chair crushed against the wall. But it could very easily have gone quite wrong. A runaway car's steering can be affected by all kinds of minor things: the exact angle of the slope, a bit of unevenness in the ground. Anyone surreptitiously setting the car in motion could not possibly have been certain of the accuracy of the missile he had just launched.

The second question to consider, was how safe was it from detection? The answer to that was that in this category it got top marks. Short of an eyewitness, the whole thing remained an accident. And the overwhelming odds were simply that: it was an accident.

I stopped and got out to close the garden gate across the driveway and a motorcycle puttered to a stop by the kerb. I knew who the rider was before he removed his helmet and smiled at me.

'Hello. Are you going painting?'

'Not really. Not today.' I walked over to his motorcycle in an easy gesture of friendliness. I wanted a look at those tyres, though I had no doubt what I would see.

'You're limping,' Liam Stuart said concernedly.

He said something else which I didn't hear because I was staring at the tyres of his hired motorbike. The treads on those tyres had not left the tracks I had seen behind a bush on the Norrises' road.

Not Liam. So who was the watcher with the binoculars? An innocent bird-watcher? Innocent bird-watchers hid themselves from birds sometimes, but they did not hide their motorcycles.

'Are you all right?' Liam was asking anxiously.

I looked up quickly. 'Oh, sorry, I was — thinking of something else.'

'So I gathered. You looked as though it might be something bad. Was it?'

'No.' I smiled suddenly. 'No, it wasn't bad.' I couldn't say: I thought you were spying on me, or on the Norrises. And if you were, I thought – God knows what I thought, but it was ugly. And I was wrong, and that isn't bad, Mr Stuart. That isn't bad at all.

'Before you went off into your little reverie,' he said, looking gently amused, 'I was asking what had happened to your foot or leg or whatever. When you got out of the car you were limping.'

I told him. I didn't intend to tell him, but suddenly it was a tremendous relief to be able to talk about it. Not, of course, to tell him I was fearful it could have been attempted murder; nothing about frantic notes begging for help. I simply called it an accident.

He listened seriously. 'It took a lot of guts to do what you did,' he said. 'You might have had a lot more than a bruised leg.'

I shrugged. 'There's no question of heroics. You're only brave if you do something in spite of being afraid to do it. I wasn't afraid because there wasn't time to be afraid. It was just a reaction.'

'Uh-huh.' He seemed to consider for a moment. 'This old lady – the aunt. Is she *compos mentis*?'

'Oh, yes. Very much so, I'd say. When she's sober.'

'I see. And yesterday? Was she sober then?'

I shook my head. 'She'd made a point of telling me, one day, that she never drove when she'd been drinking. But yesterday she did, I'm afraid.' I frowned. 'Something happened to upset her, I'm sure – something while she was out shopping. Because I felt she really took pride in her driving ability and wouldn't impair it by drinking when she knew she had to drive.'

'Well, that's what happens to alcoholics, you know: something goes wrong – it might be something as insignificant as a parking-ticket or a shop having already sold a dress she'd decided to buy – whatever it might be, they have a drink for consolation. And another and another. I gather the lady *is* an alcoholic?'

'I'm afraid so.' I smiled. 'She said the family calls her eccentric because it sounds better.'

He grinned. 'An interesting family, these friends of yours.'

'Well, they're not really friends. I'd never met them before – it's just that I wanted to paint there, and they allowed me, very kindly, to do it.'

I thought of the watcher in the trees. *Someone* finds them very interesting, I thought. Or – with a quick involuntary shiver – someone finds *me* interesting. And being surreptitiously watched with binoculars was not the sort of interest anyone welcomed.

'Well,' Liam said, 'I came to ask if you'd come with me for a picnic lunch at a spot I should think any artist would like to paint. There's a place in town that puts up picnic lunch-boxes. It mightn't be the Ritz but the food's not bad at all. And of course,' he added with that schoolboy grin, 'the company is charming.'

'Of course,' I said drily. Then I smiled. 'Thanks. I think I'd like that. But first, I want to go out and see how Vi Norris is this morning. I think she might have a kind of delayed-shock reaction. And Edith Wishart was very upset yesterday over what happened. It would be a bit discourteous not to go out and see how they are.'

And see if after-shock can wring anything out of anyone. One last try.

'Let me drive you,' Liam said. 'You look as if that leg is hurting.'

It was, rather, but having Liam around would kill off any chance Vi might talk to me.

'I'm fine. I won't be away long. I'll be back in plenty of time for lunch.'

Ivan and a repair man were assessing damage when I arrived. The smashed furniture had been cleared away, a broken shrub or two pruned back hard to give them a chance to shoot again. Ivan looked up and came forward in welcome.

'How's that leg? I should have phoned, but it all seems to

have been rather hectic this morning, with insurance people, and the smash-repair people towing Aunt Edith's car away. Are you all right?'

'I'm all right, thanks. It was only a bruise. I wondered how Vi is this morning – delayed shock or something could hit today. And I'm sure Mrs Wishart is still very upset.'

He smiled ruefully. 'Yes, I think she feels much worse than Vi, actually. But go around to the kitchen – I think that's where Vi is. She's fine, but she'll be pleased to see you. And Lyn,' he added as I began to walk away, 'thank you. For yesterday. It isn't much to say. But thank you.'

I lifted a hand in acknowledgement and dismissal of the subject and went in search of Vi.

She greeted me with what I felt for the first time was genuine warmth. She was busy about the stove and I sat on a stool at the kitchen bench.

'Vi,' I said seriously, 'yesterday when we were picking ourselves up I asked you what might have sounded like a very strange question.'

She had been cooking apples, apparently for a pie, and she lifted the saucepan from the stove and seemed waiting for me to go on.

I did. 'I asked you who was trying to kill you.'

She looked at me quickly. 'Good Lord! Did you? I didn't even notice.' She laughed. 'You must have been in quite a state – and I don't wonder. But don't worry about it. We all say odd things in a moment of shock. It didn't bother me, because I didn't even hear it. Which shows the state *I* was in.'

I felt a swift surge of anger. You stupid, stubborn fool of a woman! I wanted to shout. Can't you trust me even now?

But looking at her as she chatted about yesterday's accident while she mixed pastry dough, I felt it wasn't a matter of not trusting me. Whatever had made her once fear for her life, it now no longer worried her – for whatever reason – or else she was certain yesterday's happening had no possible relevance to her other fears. I wondered if she would feel the same if she had known about the watcher beside the road.

Certainly she hadn't escaped as unperturbed as she wanted to pretend. She was too talkative, her hands so unsteady she fumbled over perfectly routine tasks.

But confiding her fears in me, if she had any fears to confide, was not on the agenda. I declined coffee and left. I walked up to Edith Wishart's door and knocked.

Before she opened it I knew by her footsteps she was drunk, and when I saw her I saw she was very drunk indeed.

'Oh,' she said. 'It's you. Hello. You're all right, aren't you?' The words were abrupt, but there was nothing unfriendly in her manner.

'Yes,' I said. 'I'm all right. Don't worry about it.'

'What?' She seemed to have difficulty in grasping what I may have been talking about. 'Oh, the accident. No. No point in worrying about it. That's what they all say. I'd ask you in, but I'm drunk.'

'It doesn't matter,' I assured her.

'If I'd known you were coming –' She shook her head. 'I wish I wasn't so drunk. Because I think you're all right. But I'm too drunk, damn it. Come back another day.'

'Of course,' I said. 'I will.' I looked at her closely. 'Mrs Wishart, is there something wrong?'

Blue eyes swept me searchingly, struggling with the fog of alcohol in her brain. 'I wish I knew.' The hand clutching the doorpost for steadiness tightened convulsively. 'I wish to *God* I knew.'

There was something so intense about the way she said it that I caught my breath. 'Knew what?' I asked, trying to keep her mind on whatever track it had been following.

But she seemed to have lost the thread. 'I'm drunk,' she said. 'Where's Peter?'

'I haven't seen him. Studying, I suppose.'

'Is that teacher fellow there?'

'Arnold Bright? I haven't seen his car. I don't think so.'

'He was there, you know,' she said, almost conspiratorially.

'Was he?' I was simply trying to humour her. 'Well, perhaps he had to leave. After all, it's a school day: he'd have to be at work.'

'I don't mean today,' she said contemptuously. 'The other time. But I think he might be all right.'

I stared. 'Do you mean yesterday? When the car rolled down the hill?'

But already she was thinking of something else. 'I'm not related to Ivan, you know,' she said. 'My husband was his mother's brother. You remember that.'

'Mrs Wishart,' I said in a quick, low voice, 'did you see Arnold Bright around your car yesterday? Before it rolled down the hill?'

'What?' The brain had slipped out of gear again as well. 'Oh, yesterday. The car. Peter wasn't there, was he?' Suddenly she caught my arm with her free hand while the other clutched the doorpost. 'I didn't see him. He wasn't there, was he?'

'*Peter*?' I gulped. She couldn't suspect *Peter* had launched the car on its potentially lethal roll? It would have been difficult from a wheelchair, but maybe not impossible. I felt a wave of nausea swell up in me, and then she was saying anxiously, 'Peter wasn't hurt, was he? They all said he wasn't, but I haven't seen him.'

'Oh,' I said with enormous relief. 'No, Peter wasn't hurt. He was out in the kitchen making himself a sandwich.'

'Ah.' She relaxed and released my arm. 'Good.'

'Mrs Wishart, what did you mean when you said Arnold was there?'

'Well, he was.' She shook her head. 'But I think he's all right. I really do.'

'Did you see Arnold Bright tampering with your car yesterday?' I demanded.

'Oh, they were all trying to get it going again, but it was too badly smashed. It had to be towed away. I was a bit drunk, you know. I never drive when I've been drinking. Only yesterday. I left it in neutral on that slope. I'm going to lie down. I'm a bit dizzy.'

I wasn't going to get any coherent sense out of her. 'All right,' I said gently. 'Have a rest. And I don't think you should drink any more today. Please.'

She patted my arm. 'Come back when I'm more nearly

sober. I like you.'

I smiled. 'I like you, too,' I said.

For a moment the blue eyes were clear and bright. 'Thank you, my dear. You're all right, aren't you?'

And she closed the door.

And for the first time I realized that her use of the words 'all right' didn't mean physically undamaged. They meant something else: honest; trustworthy. Not involved in – what? What did she believe was happening in this household? It might be no more than some minor trifle she was magnifying as an excuse for reaching for consolation in a bottle. But as I drove back towards town I had a gnawingly uneasy feeling that whatever was troubling Edith Wishart was not a trifle.

Liam was right when he said the spot he had in mind for a picnic was one almost any landscape painter would find fascinating – especially one like me who found sunlight which glittered on water and back-lit overhanging trees presented an almost irresistible challenge. The shallow river in its pebbly bed was just a few metres wide here as it swept gently around a bend where willows in autumn gold dress scattered bright leaves on ripple-reflected sunlight. A wooden bridge formed a backdrop and, to prevent it being too chocolate-box pretty, a great dead eucalypt beside the bridge raised its bleached skeleton above the ruins of what had once been a stone cottage – the wreckage of someone else's dreams now reduced to a crumbling chimney and some remnants of broken wall amid a tangle of blackberries.

I looked at it in silence for what I think was probably quite a long time. When I turned Liam was watching me with a gentle smile that was quite unlike the mischievous grin that made him look so boyish.

'It's – beautiful,' I said.

He held out his arms and I went into them as naturally as if I had done so a hundred times, and our kiss was long and very far from casual.

Presently I turned, with his arms still around me, to look

back at the river. 'I only hope I can paint it properly,' I said a trifle shakily. 'It will always be my special place – *our* place.'

'Hey,' he said softly, kissing the top of my head. 'Our place? That's dangerous talk.'

'Do you mind?'

'Not at all,' he said. And for rather a long time we lost interest in the river completely, and an intoxicating mix of fire and gentleness threw away all pretence that ours was just a casual friendship.

Later, as we sat on the rug he had brought and ate our picnic lunch, we chatted easily. He talked about his boyhood on his family's farm in northern Victoria, and of how he had loved to go hiking and camping in the hills.

'Hunting, I suppose?' I said.

Maybe he caught some inflection in my voice that betrayed my dislike of the idea, because he looked at me quickly. 'No,' he said. 'I never did like hunting. Funny, that,' he added musingly, 'considering –' He stopped and shrugged. 'Maybe I'll have to go back, after this.'

'To farming? But surely that would be much harder to handle than a public service job – after your accident, I mean.'

'Yes. Well, I'll just have to see how it works out.'

'Do you still have much pain from your injuries?'

'Not that much.' He grinned. 'Ever since my outdoors-loving youth I've managed to stay pretty fit. That helps.'

'I think as a boy you must have been rather like Peter,' I smiled.

'Peter? Oh, the crippled boy at the Norrises you were telling me about. Was he an outdoors type before his accident?'

I nodded. 'He'd totally set his heart on being a wildlife photographer – the best in the world, he told me. It's such a terrible *waste*, to see him like that now. Because he had a future as a photographer, no question. He showed me some of his work yesterday, and it's good – it would be very good for anyone. For a thirteen year old it's completely exceptional. Some of the photographs are small works of art in themselves. I remember –' I broke off. Liam was staring at the ground, a look of sheer pain on his face.

'I'm sorry,' I said. 'I've made you think of your own accident.'

'No, not really. It just comes back, sometimes. When I don't expect it.'

He had withdrawn, thrown up a wall between us. Not knowing whether it was the right or wrong thing to do, I had a quick shot at knocking it down.

'In your accident, were you – the only one hurt?'

'No.' He had pulled a grass straw and was running it through his fingers again and again. 'Someone was killed.'

'Your wife?' I asked gently.

He turned his head to look at me for a moment. 'No,' he said, and there was a silence.

'I'm sorry,' I said again. 'I had no right to go prying.'

He played with the grass straw for a minute or two and then tossed it away and reached out to put his hand over mine.

'It's all right. One day I'll tell you about it. One day I'll have to. And your guess was partly right: I did lose my wife. But that was four years ago, and it wasn't an accident. She died of cancer. We'd been married less than a year.'

'I'm a clumsy fool,' I said. 'Try to forgive me.'

He shook his head. 'There's nothing to forgive. And I can think about it now without wanting to blow my brains out. Her name was Kate and she was tall and red-haired and laughed a lot and I loved her. When she was dying she told me that when she was gone I was to say goodbye and get on with living. I wonder sometimes if she knew how hard that would be. But she knew, and I know now, that it had to be done. No matter how much it hurt.'

We sat in silence for a while, but it was a silence without awkwardness.

'What about you?' he asked presently.

'Me?'

'Mmm. Husband?'

'No.'

'Lover?'

'Went to Western Australia and lost my address.'

'Oh. Well, let's have done with the gloom. Have another sandwich.'

'I couldn't. Let's pack the picnic things away and go for a walk.'

'You have an injured leg.'

'A short walk would do it good. Let's go on to the bridge and play Pooh-sticks.'

'Play what?'

'Didn't you ever read *Winnie The Pooh* when you were a child?'

He roared laughing. 'Here I am out with a one-day-she'll-be-famous artist and she wants to play about the most basic kids' game in the world.'

We played Pooh-sticks and ducks-and-drakes and laughed a great deal in the sun, and for a little while I escaped totally into another world, an innocent world far removed from anguished notes and runaway cars and alcoholic elderly ladies and fathers with terrible secrets; even from gifted boys in wheelchairs.

It was as we walked back to the car – slowly, both reluctant I think, to take up harsh realities again – that Liam asked, 'What's Peter's name?'

'Peter?'

'I can't help thinking of him in that wheelchair instead of out playing like other kids – even walking along the river bank like we're doing now. I know there are a lot of kids in wheelchairs, but it doesn't really hit you until you come across one yourself. He's not the Norrises' son, is he?'

'No. A son of Vi's cousin. His name's Fisher.'

Liam drove me home. As he stopped the car outside the cottage he leaned over and kissed me gently. 'I'm glad that idiot went to Western Australia,' he said. 'Come to dinner with me again tonight?'

'I can't,' I said. 'I'm having dinner with friends.'

And at once the whole weight of everything that had been pushed into the background for a few hours crashed over me again like a massive surf swamping an unwary swimmer. With it came the knowledge that one day, unless

I greatly misunderstood what was happening between us, I would have to tell Liam what I had had to tell Eric. And perhaps he would go to Western Australia or its equivalent distance, too.

'Tomorrow night?' he was saying. 'Please?'

Alice Duer-Miller's lines came into my head again:

So I put my gloved hand into his glove,
And we danced together – and fell in love.

'Tomorrow night,' I smiled.

Before the dream ends and I have to tell him, I thought.

Dinner at the Miller household was, as I had expected, not the most relaxed of meals.

Sally had not given me any indication of her children's reaction to the news that their stepfather was a convicted murderer. I felt great sympathy for them, though I felt, too, that I mustn't show it. They didn't have the insulation of childhood trust that I'd had when I found out: the shining faith that had made me shout angrily that everyone was wrong. The love of my father that had somehow survived the years of my mother's bitterness against him, survived the reality of knowing the known facts. Survived – not unscathed, certainly – somehow struggling through in rags tattered by the truth, still in enough strength to send me out to find him, even though that search was fuelled principally by the need to know more about the balance of good and evil in the man who was my father.

While Sally's children didn't have that buffer of ever having loved Roger with the uncritical innocence of childhood to protect them against the shock of the truth, they had the advantage I didn't have: they knew him as he was *now*; they stood in a better position to assess him. But at the moment anger probably overrode cool, analytical judgments.

From the moment Sally showed me into the house it was clear that her children had each reacted very differently. It was quite probable, I realized, that they had always had differing attitudes to Roger's entry into their lives.

Sally smiled at me a shade nervously as she met me at the door, looking drawn and pale, but attractive in a soft blue jumper and a well-cut grey checked skirt, a silver chain necklet her only ornament.

'I'm so glad you came,' she said quietly. 'Please try to bear with us. You've hurt your leg,' she added quickly. 'You're limping.'

'It's only a bruise. I'll tell you about it later.'

Then we were in the sitting-room, and I had a vague impression of a pleasant room, tastefully furnished and looking comfortably lived-in. But any impressions of the decor were completely overriden by my need to assess the people.

A fire burned cheerfully in the fireproof-glass-doored slow-combustion heater and Roger stood beside it, hands behind his back, watching me unsmilingly as I came in, his eyes expressionless in that deliberate retreat from displaying any kind of emotion I had come to know.

In the chair farthest from the door a boy perhaps a year older than Peter slouched back, eyes intent on a book – a strongly-built boy, brown-haired and very like Sally, not tall, but looking as if he played a lot of sport. He was dressed in worn-out sneakers, grubby jeans and raggy sweater, his hair uncombed; everything about him a defiant gesture of protest. He didn't glance up from his book, but I doubted if he was seeing a word on the page in front of him.

Clearly the two male members of the family were here only on sufferance.

Not so the girl who turned quickly from rearranging a vase of fern and violets that stood on a coffee-table. Tall, slender, fair-haired, she was about seventeen, dressed in close-fitting black pants, a white blouse with lace demurely at the throat, and an outrageously voluminous red knitted jacket.

Green eyes sparkling, she came to meet me with both hands outstretched. 'Hello, Lyn. I'm Rosemary.' She took my hands, kissed my cheek lightly and easily, and stepped back to sweep a frankly appraising glance over me. 'Isn't this exciting? I have a stepsister. Oh, dear, does that make you sound like something out of *Cinderella?* Sorry. I think it's marvellous. I've been dying to meet you. Mummy says you're an artist. Do you have any of your paintings with you? I'd love to see some.'

She went on while I stood smiling, letting the torrent of her enthusiasm pour over me, accepting its warmth gratefully, but still aware that beyond Rosemary the room almost crackled with antagonism. I don't think she was unaware of it, and indeed I felt that she was deliberately trying to insulate me a little from it.

Brent cut in, 'Shut up, Rosemary. I want my dinner.'

Rosemary flashed me an apologetic smile. 'That's my brother, oozing charm over there. Lyn, meet Brent.' He lifted his head, rebellious hazel eyes meeting mine in a hostile stare. 'Brent *Watson*,' he said firmly, in a clear statement that the contamination of the Sutton-Miller names did not rub off on him. 'Hello,' he added grudgingly, and I felt that ill manners were not his normal behaviour.

'Hi, Brent. Hello, Roger.'

Roger nodded briefly and Sally said with a gallant effort to make it seem a normal, casual evening, 'Roger, would you fix a drink for Lyn while I see to dinner? I'm sure everything will be ready.'

Almost in silence Roger poured me a sherry and waved me to a chair, while Rosemary continued to chatter easily and Brent stayed buried in his book. Without appearing to watch him, I could see from the corner of my eye he didn't turn a single page.

Dinner made a fair pretence of being a normal meal, thanks primarily to Sally and Rosemary, who kept conversation moving easily enough in uncontroversial paths. We talked of gardening and the differences in climate between my sub-tropical home and here; of the Miller family pets – a dog and two cats; of school – Rosemary was in her final year of high school. Brent, when I asked him a direct question, said he had two more years to do. 'If I go on with it,' he added sullenly. No one enlarged on that with any comment, so I gathered it was a new idea, another protest against the situation, and everyone felt it was best ignored. I told them, withholding certain details, how I came to injure my leg, and that led to talk about my painting.

'I really admire artistic people,' Rosemary said, 'though I haven't a shred of artistic talent myself. I'm going to do law.'

'With a stepfather who's done time in the slammer that should give you a head start,' Brent said acidly.

'That's enough, Brent.' Sally kept her voice quiet and calm.

'Oh, for God's sake!' Brent exploded. 'Why are we playing this fool game? What is it supposed to be? Happy Families? Father Knows Best?'

'We're not playing games,' his mother said. 'Lyn is a part of our family, and we should get to know her, and she has a right to get to know us.'

'She's not part of *my* family!' he snapped, rage and hurt out of control in him. 'No bloody Miller or Sutton or whatever they want to call themselves is part of my family.'

He leapt up from the table, pushing back his chair.

'Sit down, Brent,' Roger ordered curtly.

'Don't you try to tell me what to do!' He wheeled and strode toward the door. He had to come around to my side of the table to reach the door he wanted, and almost without thinking I stood and stepped in front of him.

'Can I come with you? I'd like a chance to talk.'

'Go to hell!' he said, and pushed past me.

'Let him go,' Rosemary said. 'He's just being a pig.'

I shook my head. 'No,' I said. 'He's just being normal.'

'He's right, of course,' Roger said heavily. 'We're playing some kind of damn-fool charade.'

'What we're trying to do,' Sally put in, 'is get on with living our lives. That's what we have to do. It's reality. It isn't any kind of charade.' She was white-faced and looked as if she had aged ten years since I walked in the door. She could see her family disintegrating around her, fight as she would to prevent it.

I looked at my father. 'Roger, will you please do something for all of us?'

He looked at me suspiciously, eyes narrowed. 'Like go out and hang myself?'

'I'm going to try to persuade Brent to come back. And then I want you to tell us, once and for all, what happened that night.'

He turned his back on me to stare at the fire. 'Read the old newspapers. They tell it all.'

'That's rubbish and you know it. We know you broke into the jewellers': in that, you were guilty and the jury and the papers got it right. We don't know whether you killed the night-watchman. If you didn't, I want you to say so. If you did, I want you to tell us why – just how it happened. Because you haven't forgotten. You wouldn't forget any of it – every move, everything you felt – not in two hundred years, let alone twenty.'

'I've told you before –'

'When I get Brent, you can tell us. You're the one who called this a charade. Very well. End the play. Which is Brent's room?'

There was a tiny silence. 'Second on your left,' Rosemary said, looking almost awed.

I went into the hall, knowing that if I stopped to think what I was doing I probably wouldn't go on with it. In answer to my knock, a tape-recorder was turned on very loudly. I tried the handle and found the door wasn't locked. Brent was lying on his bed, staring at the ceiling.

'Go away,' he said.

I walked over and switched the player off. 'Come into the lounge. Roger has something to say to us.'

'Then he can say it without me.'

'Brent, if you don't come into that room now, it's going to be much harder tomorrow. You'll have put a gulf between your mother and yourself and it will get harder and harder to bridge.'

'I'm not doing anything to hurt Mum.'

'But you are. She wants to sort this whole thing out, to find out whether you can make a go of it as a family unit.'

'With him in it?'

'Didn't you like him? Before, I mean?'

Brent shrugged. 'He was all right.'

'He's still the same person.'

'You mean he never was the person we thought he was.'

'Not one of us is ever quite the person other people think we are. We're probably not quite the people *we* think we are. We can only judge people by the way they are now, for us.'

I paused. 'I'm sorry. I'm putting all this badly. But it matters an awful lot to me, too. I'm asking Roger to tell us what happened, that night. I think he might. Will you please come out and hear it for yourself?'

'I know what happened.' He wasn't looking at me.

'No, you don't. No one but Roger knows what happened. Let's give it a try and take it from there. OK?'

'Oh, OK. I can't see what you're trying to prove, but OK.'

We went out to the lounge together. The others were still and silent, Sally and Rosemary sitting on the couch, Roger still standing by the fire. Brent flung himself into the chair he'd occupied before dinner. I went over and stood beside my father.

'Roger, did you kill that night-watchman?'

'What good –'

'Did you?'

There was a long, frozen silence. I could hear my own pulse pounding in my ears. Roger turned and looked at me wearily, then looked across at Sally.

'No,' he said.

'Bully for innocence established,' Brent said. 'Can I go now?'

'What happened?' I persisted, not taking my eyes off Roger.

'The place was done over,' he said. 'All I got was that bloody pendant. When I was leaving, I found the security-patrol guy. He was very dead and the Stilsons were beside him. No need to wonder what he died of. I bolted for home. I remember I vomited three times on the way. It was only next day I remembered I'd left a drill up in the ceiling, and it had my name on it. As a break-and-enter merchant I guess I was doomed to have a very short career.'

He was very still and silent for a moment. 'Well,' he said finally, 'there you have my version of it.'

'What's it supposed to prove?' Brent demanded. 'It's just words.'

'Exactly,' Roger said. He looked around the room. 'No word of this goes outside this house. Does everyone understand that?'

'Of course,' Rosemary said. Sally and I nodded.

Brent sneered, 'You think we want anyone to know what suckers we've been? No one's going to go around blabbing that sort of muck.'

'Why did you keep the pendant?' I asked.

He glanced at me. 'The final nail in my coffin? I guess I was in a state of shock. I simply forgot I had it. I wouldn't have known how to sell it, anyway.'

'Shock is pretty understandable,' Rosemary said with quite a degree of sympathy. 'Robbery wasn't good, but to find you were mixed up in a murder you had nothing to do with – that was horrible for you.'

'Don't tell me you believe that cock-and-bull story!' Brent said scornfully.

'Why shouldn't I?'

'Hans Christian Andersen couldn't have dreamed up more of a fairy story than that.'

Roger was watching his wife, who sat silently staring at her hands gripped together in her lap.

'Sally?'

She raised her eyes to his. I do not expect ever to feel more sorry for another human being. 'Why did you do it? Try to rob the jewellery store?'

He shrugged. 'Sheer greed. I'd worked on the building. I knew how to get in through the roof without triggering alarms. I figured the stuff would be covered by insurance and I told myself no one would really be any worse off. In one night I could get stuff worth years of what I could earn by hard work. There was some risk, I knew. That only made it more exciting. I was young. And *bloody* stupid.'

'The watchman.' She spoke as though her throat was painful. 'Where – was he hit from in front or from behind?'

Roger's face was impassive, but his eyes were intent on her. 'From behind.'

'Then you didn't kill him.' She got up and went to him, holding out her hands, and he took them.

'Brilliant detective work, Mum.' Brent's voice was still venomous with sarcasm. 'How'd you work that out?'

'Roger might have struck out and killed a man who had come face to face with him suddenly. But I cannot believe he could strike down an unsuspecting man from behind.'

'Bull,' said Brent.

'*I* think Mummy's right,' declared Rosemary. 'You *read* about things like that happening, but you never expect to meet someone it's happened to. You got a rotten deal, Roger.' She went over and kissed his cheek lightly. Brent stormed out of the room.

Roger had drawn Sally's arm through his and was holding her hand tightly as if he were afraid she might evaporate like some lovely dream. 'Nothing changes the fact I'm a thief,' he said, looking at me.

'You *were* a thief,' I responded. 'What have you stolen since?'

He gave the faintest hint of a smile. 'A few packets of cigarettes while I was inside.'

'I think I can live with that. I think we all can live with that. Thieves can change.'

'But not murderers?'

'I – don't know. I guess it depends on the kind of murder.'

'Do you think I'm a murderer?'

I suddenly felt a most dreadful intruder in this household. Two for, one against.

'I don't know.' One undecided.

'That is precisely what I told you in the first place: you wouldn't know. If I told you I was guilty you'd believe me fast enough.'

I was silent, knowing he was right.

'Did you expect me to tell you, tonight, that I was a murderer?'

'I didn't know what to expect. I thought if you had killed the security man you might tell us exactly how it happened.'

'So you'd know what kind of murder it was? Spur-of-the-moment panic, or calculating cold blood. So then you'd know whether I was reformed or not. God preserve me from the amateur psychologist.'

He kept his voice quiet and steady, but the bitter anger was just below the surface.

'Would you mind,' he said in the same tone, 'going home now?'

I turned without a word and walked to the door, because there seemed to be nothing more I could say or do to repair the disastrous damage I had brought to his family.

'Lyn!' Sally said quickly. 'Roger, this is my home, too, and Lyn is your daughter. I will not have you order her to leave.'

I paused. 'It's all right, Sally. I'll go. I've done enough damage. I'm sorry.'

'She can come back,' Roger said thickly, 'another time. If she wants to. Right now I want to be left alone.'

'Will you, Lyn?' Sally asked. 'Come back?'

I looked at them. 'I came here to try to get to know my father,' I said eventually. 'I guess that hasn't changed. I'll come back, if you'll have me.'

And I hurried away to a night when sleep was hard to come by.

Seven

In the morning I walked into the town for no particular reason except that I felt I needed to walk to clear my muddled brain and I hoped the exercise would loosen the stiffness in my bruised leg. My night had been filled with joyful memories of the hours beside the river with Liam, and wretched memories of the scenes inside the Miller household. Today was overcast with a chill wind, and I thought some exercise might help keep its greyness from seeping into my soul.

When the motorcycle muttered to a stop beside me, I had no doubt who it was and I turned with a smile. 'You're just –'

I stopped. It wasn't Liam, but Roger Miller who was taking off his helmet to look at me with hostile eyes.

'Well,' he said without preamble, 'are you satisfied now with what you've done? We were a happy family unit before you came. Now my wife looks at me with an unanswered question in her mind and maybe wonders if she's safe. Rosemary thinks there's something glamorous about having been in prison and one day is going to wake up to what it was all about and be afraid of me. And Brent hates me. You've really done us all a power of good, haven't you?'

'Don't you realize they were going to find out eventually?' I countered. 'It's easy to blame me, but I didn't come here to destroy anything. I didn't seek them out and tell them your history, remember. Sally came looking for me because she realized there was something wrong. And even then –'

I stopped, staring.

'Well?' he said, looking down at his bike, evidently startled by the expression on my face. 'What's wrong?'

'It's just — I didn't know you rode a motorbike.' A red and white motorcycle like Liam's hired one. A motorcycle with tyres whose tread had left that pattern I had seen in mud on the side of Norrises' road. A motorcycle whose rider had watched the Norris house with binoculars.

'It's a quick way of going somewhere to do a quote or something where I don't need all my plumbing gear.' He was looking at me curiously. 'Are you all right?'

Somehow the note of concern in his voice was such a contrast to his accusing bitterness of a moment before that for an unguarded moment I was close to tears.

'Yes,' I said. 'It's just that I came here to try to sort out a part of my life that otherwise was always going to be an enigma. I came here to get to know you. Now I don't believe I ever will.'

I walked away. It was quite some seconds before I heard him kick his motorcycle into life and ride on.

Waves of new questions were sweeping through my brain. I had been followed a number of times — whether deliberately or not, admittedly, I didn't know for sure — by a red and white motorcycle which until yesterday I had, in an uneasy puzzle, assumed was Liam's. Had it been Roger who followed me, and if so, why on earth had he done so? Had it been Roger who watched the Norris house with binoculars? Almost certainly. It was a little too much to ask of coincidence that it had been a stranger whose tyre-treads just happened to be of the same pattern.

Why had Roger Miller been watching the Norris house? Was his interest in someone in their household? Or in me? Why did he care that much what I did? I sighed and walked on. All my mental twists and turns only produced more questions and not a single answer. The car stopping beside me didn't register until Liam spoke.

'Lyn, I've been looking for you.' He got out of the car and came around to me. 'You don't look awfully well. Why are you walking? That leg must be hurting.'

He took both my hands and stood looking at me with a concerned little smile. I wanted to fling myself into his arms and pour out my troubles.

Instead I said, 'Oh, I felt blue and thought a walk might do us both good – me and my leg.'

'It looks as if it might rain. Let me drive you. It does not really look to me as if walking is doing either you or your leg much good. Where do you want to go?'

'I wasn't really going anywhere – just walking.' I glanced up at the darkening sky. 'It does look like rain. I may as well go home, if you don't mind. Can you stop in for coffee?'

'The only other thing on my social programme around here is fish, and they run a bad second.' He was trying to sound flippant, but there was a seriousness in his face and I felt I wasn't the only one with troublesome thoughts.

'That certainly makes me feel important,' I said with my own attempt at lighthearted banter which fell even flatter.

As we drove back toward the cottage he glanced at me. 'Painting not turning out the way you want?'

'Painting? Oh. Well, I don't suppose it ever does, not really. Perhaps that's not a bad thing at all. Maybe when you think you've really got it right, you should give up, because that means you think you know it all, and when you think that, you've lost everything that made it worthwhile.'

He nodded. 'I guess that applies to every profession.'

We drove the rest of the way in silence, and when we went into the cottage Liam said, 'It's chilly. I'll light the fire.'

I was a shade surprised, but only said, 'Fine. I'll go and make the coffee.'

He had a bright little fire crackling in the grate when I came back with our mugs of coffee, and he took them for me and put them on the table and drew me tightly against him and we stood in a long kiss. Then he smiled that odd little lopsided smile and said, 'Pity to let good coffee go cold.'

I gave a small slightly unsteady laugh and said, 'I can always make some more.'

But the grave look was back on his face and he handed me my coffee and we sat one on either side of the fireplace.

'Lyn, I'm afraid I have something unhappy to tell you.'

I felt my heart give a lurch of alarm and I looked at him apprehensively.

'Your friends, the Norrises. There's been a tragedy there.'

A wave of icy nausea slammed into my stomach. Vi. A woman had cried out desperately for help from a friend who wasn't there to answer. And I, poor wretched useless substitute that I was, had failed her utterly.

'Vi,' I said, barely above a whisper.

Liam watched me for a second, his eyes alert. 'No. Not Vi. Edith Wishart.'

I just stared at him for a moment, too shocked to comprehend, and I must have looked as numb as I felt, because he reached across and took the mug of coffee from me and put it on the table.

'Aunt Edith,' I said. Then, 'How?'

'I'm sorry, Lyn. You liked her, didn't you?'

I nodded. 'She was – quite a character. I wanted to get to know her much better. There was something about her – even though she was an alcoholic – a kind of warmth.'

Warmth, I thought. That was it – that was the thing that was missing in the rest of the Norris household, somehow; and perhaps it was only missing towards me.

I asked again. 'How? What happened?'

'She had a gas heater in her bedroom. Apparently she turned it on and forgot to light it, or changed her mind about wanting it lit and then forgot she'd turned it on, and went to bed. The window was closed, as anyone's would be on a cold night with wind and the threat of rain. She'd closed her bedroom door. It's only a small room, apparently. The rest was inevitable. She wouldn't have known anything about it,' he added gently. 'She just went to sleep and the gas made sure she didn't wake up. I gather she'd probably been drinking fairly heavily.'

I nodded silently. It was all so easy to picture. When I had seen her yesterday morning she was very drunk. While I had been out by the river falling irreparably in love with Liam Stuart, Edith Wishart, unable to deal with whatever problems life pushed across her path, had no doubt gone on getting drunker, to the point where she no longer remembered turning on the gas, or no longer remembered to light it. The scenario was easy to picture.

Liam said gently, 'I'm sorry, Lyn.'

I managed a shaky smile. 'Well, she doesn't have to try to blot life out with alcohol any more. Maybe it's what she would have wanted.'

I reached for my coffee and found it was cold. I must have been sitting thinking of Edith Wishart for longer than I realized. Liam got up and took the mug from me. 'I'll make some more,' he said.

He went out to the kitchen and a little splatter of rain gusted against the windows. I shivered and stretched my hands out to the warmth of the fire. This was why Liam had lit a fire – he had known that news of Edith Wishart's death would chill me with shock.

Shock. I thought about that for a while. In actual fact I scarcely knew Mrs Wishart, so why did her death hit me with such impact? The manner of it was a bit bizarre, certainly, but as I had just reflected it was easy to picture. Too easy?

A prickling feeling of horror literally tingled across my skin as I remembered Vi's voice, that day when they didn't know I was within earshot. 'I don't like it. She's dangerous, no matter what you say.'

Ivan had been trying to calm her, making light of her fears, rather as if they were the product of pure imagination, but Vi was unconvinced.

Had it been Edith Wishart she'd feared? And if so, did she fear malice or drunken bumbling constituted the danger?

Well, events, had proved Mrs Wishart was dangerous, in fact. First, dangerous to anyone who happened to be in the way when she left her car parked in neutral on a slope that turned it into a deadly projectile, and with only a useless hand-brake to restrain it. And now, dangerous indeed to herself. But there was no malice there, only drunken bumbling.

Or that was how it appeared.

But suppose Vi Norris believed the runaway car was not an accident? It had looked like one. Poor Aunt Edith, too drunk to know what she was doing. So if it was followed by another accident – poor Aunt Edith, too drunk to know what she was doing – who would question it?

If you were afraid someone was trying to kill you, and that person was fast asleep in a drunken stupor and wouldn't hear even if you stamped around the room in hobnailed boots, and the room was small and there was a gas heater – Turn on the gas; make sure the window was tightly closed; shut the door and leave quietly so no one outside saw or heard you. Problem solved.

'She's dangerous.' Well, she wasn't dangerous now.

I shuddered, *Vi*? Was it possible? First a panic-stricken cry for help and then, because that help didn't come, take the ultimately desperate measure – the final solution? Was Vi capable of doing that?

I couldn't know that. I didn't know her well enough to make that kind of assessment. I doubted whether one could ever know anyone well enough to know what they would do in a state of sheer desperation. I didn't know whether my own father could take a heavy wrench and bash a night-watchman's head in. I certainly couldn't guess whether a woman I'd only recently met could be driven by fear to murder an elderly lady.

'Lyn?'

I looked up quickly. Liam was standing there holding out my mug of fresh coffee, and I suspected he'd had to speak twice before I registered his presence.

'Oh, sorry. I was thinking.'

'I noticed.' He sat down in the other chair. 'Lyn, when I told you there'd been a tragedy at the Norris place, you said: "Vi". Why did you think something had happened to Mrs Norris?'

The question caught me off-guard and I suspected he meant to do just that. He was watching me keenly with those dark blue eyes – alert, curious.

I sipped the hot coffee and looked at the fire. 'I don't know, really,' I lied. 'I suppose – it was because I'd been

concerned for her, having had that close call with the car
running down the hill.'

'They do seem,' he said drily, 'to be an accident-prone
household.'

'Liam,' I said presently as a thought occurred to me, 'how
did you know about Mrs Wishart?'

'A friend of mine is a police sergeant here. I'd gone up to
the station to have a word with him when they got the call. I
gather Mrs Norris went to Mrs Wishart's flat to see if she was
all right.' He bent down and tossed more wood on the fire.
'It must have been a pretty nasty shock, on top of the bad
fright she got the day before yesterday.'

'Yes,' I said.

'Were they particularly close – Mrs Wishart and Mrs
Norris?'

'I don't really know them well enough to judge,' I
answered carefully. 'Mrs Wishart wasn't Vi's aunt, of
course; she was Ivan's, and even then only an aunt by
marriage.'

A point she had been anxious to make to me only
yesterday. 'I'm not related to Ivan, you know,' she had told
me while she struggled to think through a haze of alcohol.
'You remember that.' Why had it seemed important to her?
How did one follow drunken reasoning?

'You were talking to her yesterday,' Liam went on. 'How
did she seem?'

'Edith?'

He nodded.

'She was very drunk.'

'I know. You told me that. But you also said she'd been
drinking the day before, which no doubt was why she'd left
her car parked badly. Did you get the impression that she
was worried about something?'

I looked at him sharply. 'What do you mean?'

But for the first time my mind looked in the direction his
had been following. 'That sounds to me like the sort of
question your policeman friend would ask. Isn't it? "Was the
deceased in your opinion in a disturbed state of mind?" You
think she might have committed *suicide*?' I felt a touch of

anger, and I guess it showed up in my voice.

'Lyn,' he said quietly, 'I don't know what happened. But there'll almost certainly be a Coroner's enquiry and you may very well be asked to appear at it and answer questions as one of the last people to see her alive. The question of suicide has to be looked at.'

'And the question of foul play?'

He was still watching me, and there was a faintly puzzled look in his eyes. 'I should think that would quickly be ruled out.'

'Then what would be the point of an inquest?'

'All manner of things have to be considered, as I understand it – things like whether she was the victim of faulty equipment. I don't even know if there will be an enquiry. I was just trying to prepare you for the fact that there might be, and the possibility of suicide could certainly be raised. I wondered if she seemed particularly worried over anything.'

'I guess when an alcoholic goes on a binge it's usually because there's some worry they can't handle,' I said, my anger fading. 'Yesterday, of course, she was upset because the car could have run down and killed someone.'

I paused, not knowing whether to tell him any more, much as I wanted to. Yesterday – dear God, was it really only yesterday? – I had asked Edith Wishart if something was wrong. And she had answered: 'I wish I knew. I wish to *God* I knew.'

Knew what? I had tried to get her to tell me, but the alcohol had prevented her from following any line of thought coherently. Quite probably she could have been worried about her own health – maybe suspected she had some major illness, like cancer. Would she take her own life just because she suspected she was ill? Things like that did happen. But she'd said: 'If I'd known you were coming –' Then she had stopped for a moment and then said, 'I wish I wasn't so drunk. Because I think you're all right. But I'm too drunk, damn it. Come back another day.'

If she had known I was coming. What did she mean? I

thought she may have meant she would have stayed sober. There was some special reason she wanted to be sober, something she had wanted to talk to me about, but was too drunk to do so, or even know whether she should confide in me. Three times she had said I was 'all right' as if she were trying to be sure she could trust me. And when I was leaving she had said: 'Come back when I'm more nearly sober.'

I looked up at Liam and shook my head. 'I don't believe she killed herself. That is, I don't believe she *meant* to. She asked me, twice, to come back when she was sober. I believe she meant it. I think she wanted to talk to me about something in particular, but she was just sober enough to know she was too drunk to make sense.'

'So you think something was worrying her.'

'I don't know that worrying is quite the right word for it. I think there was something she wanted to tell me, discuss with me. But I'm also sure she intended to do just that. She was looking to some future events. Not planning to end everything.'

He nodded. 'Well, unless she left a note or something, I guess no one will ever know.'

'Death by misadventure,' I said softly.

'I guess that's what it will be put down to. It's kinder, anyway, I guess, for her family. Any children?'

'No.'

We fell silent. Death by misadventure. The phrase kept running through my brain. Twice, death by misadventure had almost claimed Vi. Now it had taken Edith Wishart. An accident-prone household indeed, as Liam had said. The terrible thing was: were they all accidents? I shivered. If Vi's panic-stricken note had been genuine, I believed there probably had been still another 'misadventure' of which she had been the target. If a killer, either from inside the household or outside it, did in fact stalk that family, then he or she was certainly skilled at making attempted murder indistinguishable from accident. That was what Vi had predicted: *It will look like an accident but it will be murder.*

But this time the victim was not Vi, therefore there could be no connection.

Except the one I didn't want to look at: Vi, convinced Aunt Edith was trying to kill her, making what military strategists call a pre-emptive strike. Not always justified.

'Do you want to go out to the Norris place?' Liam asked.

I shook my head. 'I'm not really a friend. Just someone who goes there to paint. I'd be intruding.'

He nodded. 'Glen Harlin and his wife want to meet you. I almost forgot, in all this business.'

'Who?'

'Oh, sorry. Glen and Julie Harlin – Glen's the police sergeant I know who's stationed here. I was around at their place last night and I guess I was talking about you. Julie told me I was to ask if you'd go with me to have dinner with them on Tuesday evening.'

I looked at him with a small smile. 'I had no idea you had friends here. I thought the fish and I were the only diversions.'

He grinned. 'Well, those are both pleasant ways of passing a couple of hours now and then. But, yes, I have friends here as well. I've known Glen and Julie for a long time. We were friends – lived near each other – when Kate was alive. After Kate had been gone a couple of years Julie began trying her hand at matchmaking for me. Then Glen was transferred here. I think how she feels a bit put out that I've turned up trumps at doing my own matchmaking, so she still wants to be a bit involved at getting us together.'

I put down my coffee mug rather quickly for fear my suddenly shaking hands couldn't hold it. Judging by the way I felt, I think I probably went very pale. Liam. I loved Liam. Desperately, passionately, gently, profoundly. I'd known him such a little while, but he was all I wanted.

And I would have to tell him who I was. And risk seeing shock and withdrawal in his eyes, risk having him find he suddenly had to be somewhere else, with many assurances that of course he'd be in touch right away. The sort of assurances that were a prelude to silence.

But I couldn't tell him now. Not today. In the past couple

of days I'd had enough traumas.

Tomorrow. Tomorrow I would tell him.

'Lyn, what is it?' He was beside my chair, anxiety in his voice and in his face. He took my hands and drew me to my feet. 'Have I been terribly wrong? I know we've only known each other such a little while. I wouldn't have thought it could ever happen like this, but it has – to me. I thought – desperately hoped – it was for real with you, too. Have I been terribly wrong?'

I shook my head numbly. 'You haven't been wrong. And I'd like to meet your friends.' Only known each other such a little while. Oh, Liam, you don't know anything about me at all. 'Liam,' I whispered, 'I love you.' Then his mouth silenced mine.

Tomorrow I would tell him. But today was ours, and all the tomorrows couldn't take it from us. Even though it was all they couldn't take.

Eight

I met Glen Harlin rather earlier than his wife's invitation to dinner had indicated.

He came to the cottage the day after they had found Edith Wishart dead. I was doing some weeding in the garden; a bright clear sun had banished yesterday's rain-clouds but was failing to warm my dread that yesterday's hours with Liam might well be the last we would have, once I told him who I was.

I looked up quickly as I heard the car stop at the gate, hoping and fearing it would be Liam, but at once I saw the blue light-fixture on the roof. Glen Harlin was a nice-looking dark-haired man a handful of years older than Liam and a little more heavily built. He was dressed in a neat grey business suit that stirred childhood memories of the day they had taken my father out of my life, and he was accompanied by a slim young woman in a constable's uniform.

I showed them into the house and when they were seated in the lounge I said brightly to Glen, 'You're Liam Stuart's friend. He didn't tell me you were a detective sergeant. I'd have expected to find you in uniform.'

He looked interested. 'Did you expect we'd be coming to see you?'

'Not exactly. But I guess you're here about Edith Wishart's death, and from what Liam told me there was a chance it may have been suicide. I'm not sufficiently familiar with police procedures to know whether you follow up that kind of thing.'

He nodded non-committally. 'Yes, Liam and I have been

113

friends for quite a few years. I believe Julie's asked him to bring you to dinner one night.' He smiled at me, eyes friendly. 'I hope you can come.'

I said, 'Thank you. I'd like to.' Would the invitation still stand if you knew who I was? No doubt. Anything else would be too blatantly discourteous. Would Liam take me? No doubt. For the same reason. His withdrawal from my life would be courteously unobtrusive; if it happened.

Detective Sergeant Harlin was saying he believed I'd been talking to Edith Wishart on the morning before her death. 'In fact,' he said, 'it seems you were probably the last person to see her alive.'

I must have looked surprised.

'Apparently it was not uncommon for the Norrises not to have any conversation with Mrs Wishart for a day or two. They just kept an eye out to make sure she was out and about, but I gather she lived her life quite independently from them.'

'Yes,' I agreed. 'I can imagine that would be so. But I'm not sure what I can tell you. Or why you want to know.'

He ignored the last sentence. 'When you talked to Mrs Wishart, was she in your opinion sober?'

'No.'

The young constable was writing in her notebook.

'Was there any particular reason you called on Mrs Wishart?'

'I imagine you've been told that she parked her car badly the day before and it rolled down the hill narrowly missing Vi Norris.'

'And not quite missing you, yes. The Norrises seemed quite impressed by your quick action.'

'Well, I guessed Mrs Wishart would still be upset – she was, at the time, and I felt she still would be. So I just called to see how she was.'

'And she was drunk?'

'Yes.' I found I said it reluctantly, feeling almost as if betraying a friend.

'How drunk?'

'Very. Able to walk, unsteadily; having difficulty holding

a conversation.'

'Was she drunk – in your opinion – on the day of the accident?'

I hesitated. 'Not drunk, in the accepted sense. But she admitted she had been drinking, and she was what I might term a bit tizzy.'

He looked thoughtful. 'On the last occasion when you saw her, did she seem depressed?'

The expected question. 'It's very hard to really judge a person's mind, especially when they're not sober, and I'm no psychologist.'

He smiled disarmingly. 'I'm not looking for a scientific opinion – just a normal human observation.'

I said carefully, 'I believe she was worried about something, but I have no idea what it was. If you're asking for my opinion on whether or not she was in a suicidal state of mind, the answer is no. She twice asked me to come again when she was sober. I believe she fully expected to be there when I did come back. Obviously I can't *know*, but I believe she did not commit suicide.'

'Do you believe that because you *want* to believe it?' he asked softly.

The question caught me by surprise. Was that basically why I was adamant Edith Wishart had not killed herself? Because if she had, some of the blame lay with me: I should have understood the depth of her distress better than I had.

'I suppose we never want to think someone we like felt so wretched they simply couldn't bear to go on living. But I simply think in the circumstances accident was far more likely.'

He nodded as if satisfied, and then asked conversationally, 'Did Mrs Wishart feel the cold badly?'

'I don't really know. But the weather was quite chilly enough to warrant a decision to turn the heater on.'

'Oh, yes, quite.' Glen Harlin paused for a moment as if considering whether or not to say anything more, then added, 'The deceased was wearing bedsocks. And gloves.'

I had been absently watching the constable competently

taking her notes. I swung around to look at Glen. He was watching me with interest. 'Gloves?' I echoed.

'Yes. She apparently must have suffered from cold hands.'

Gloves. So there would be no prints on the valve of the gas heater. Whether Edith had turned it on or not. And because she was wearing gloves, in the however-unlikely event someone in the police force was curious enough to check for fingerprints on that gas valve, anyone turning it on with intent to murder had a perfectly innocent explanation for the fact there were no damning prints left there: Aunt Edith had been wearing gloves.

'I see,' I said faintly.

And I did. I saw now the real reason Glen Harlin had come to see me. He was curious to know whether I could conceive of the possibility of murder. Well, now, from my reaction, he had his answer, with nothing at all written into the full and complete record of the conversation.

He nodded and both he and the constable stood up. 'Well, thanks for your time, Miss Sutton. You've been most helpful.'

Our eyes met and I think we understood each other quite well. I had swiftly developed a considerable respect for Liam's friend: he was a clever and a careful policeman.

'Sergeant,' I said quietly, 'if I *knew* anything useful, I would tell you. I didn't know Mrs Wishart long, but I liked her.'

'Yes. These tragic accidents do happen, and no doubt it's no more than an accident, but we have to make the usual routine enquiries.'

'Of course.'

They left me to my thinking.

Glen Harlin suspected murder. No, 'suspected' might be too strong a term. He wondered, that was all. Just as I had wondered, but for a different reason. I had felt uneasy because of two scraps of conversation: Vi's comment that someone – 'she' – was dangerous; and Edith's that she felt something was 'wrong'. Who was dangerous and in what way, and what was 'wrong', I couldn't know, and couldn't know whether either remark was significant. Therefore I felt I couldn't repeat them to an investigating police officer, and thus perhaps throw suspicion where none was justified.

Glen Harlin's uneasiness came from an entirely different source: Edith had worn gloves to bed. More correctly, she had been wearing gloves when the police were called. Was there anything remarkable about an elderly lady wearing gloves to keep her hands warm? She was wearing bedsocks, he had said. No one thought that odd. But the gloves had just made him curious, and I was willing to bet he had dusted that gas-valve for fingerprints and found none. So he had decided to find out whether an outsider like myself felt murder was possible in the Norris household.

I dropped in to the Millers' place unannounced. Partly because I felt that if we were ever going to be some semblance of a family unit, a casual visit on a weekend afternoon was a natural sort of thing. Partly it was because it gave me an excuse not to see Liam, and face up to telling him about my family background, and risk losing him. Telling myself that Liam was different, that he would accept me for myself, was not working.

Roger and Sally were working in the garden when I stopped the car outside and they both looked up with something like apprehension when they saw who it was, though Sally at once smiled, put down the pruning shears and came to meet me. Roger, who had been mulching some azaleas, watched me stonily.

'Hello,' I said with an attempt at casual breeziness. 'I just thought I'd drop by. No dramas. Don't interrupt your gardening. May I stay and help? I'm not totally hopeless at it, and I'm a willing worker.'

'Of course,' Sally said and, obviously understanding that I wanted to be accepted as part of the family, set me to work at some weeding, and she and I talked comfortably enough, though Roger studiously ignored me.

Rosemary came out, tennis-racket in hand, and greeted

me with enthusiasm, lamenting that she had to go, the team was expecting her. I asked Roger if Brent also played sport and he said tersely, 'He's at a soccer match. If you want any more details ask his mother. He doesn't tell me anything any more.'

'Do you ever go to watch him play?'

'I used to, if it was an important match.'

'Is this one important?'

'Fairly important.' Reluctantly.

'Then I think you should go and watch.'

'He doesn't want me to go. And I don't need you to tell me what to do and what not to do, thank you very much.'

'Roger,' I said, 'my last memory of you was of sitting on your knee while you read me a story. Before you finished the story they came and took you away. Do you think I don't bloody well know what it's like to hurt inside, and be bewildered, the way Brent feels now? Do you have any idea how long and how hard I waited for you to come back?'

I broke off quickly and turned away. 'I'm sorry. I promised not to do that. But if I were you, I'd go to that soccer match.'

I weeded furiously for a while, angry with myself for having said what I had. I was conscious of the fact that Roger stood very still for a long time. Then he turned and walked away without a word, and presently I heard the motorbike leave.

Sally, beside me, said, 'Thank you, Lyn.'

I shook my head. 'So much for my promise not to try interfering. And he probably isn't going to the soccer anyway.'

Sally smiled. 'He is. He was wearing the team scarf.'

For the rest of the afternoon our conversation was on a more general note, and we found conversation easy, a comfortable friendship growing between us. Presently we had tea and home-made fruit-cake in a sunny corner of the lounge, and for a couple of hours it was as if crime and tragedy didn't throw long chilling shadows over us both — though, in some respects, from different angles.

It was after four when I left, and I felt an acute need to

know whether anything had changed in Roger's relationship with Brent. I knew where the soccer-field was, so I drove around there on my way home, thinking I might catch sight of Roger or Brent or – hopefully – both together, even though the situation between them certainly wasn't going to repair itself in one afternoon. But if it was ever going to mend, the mending had to begin somewhere.

The playing-field was deserted except for a few enthusiastic small boys kicking a soccer ball and probably having dreams of a World Cup final. Evidently the last match of the day had just ended, because players in their soccer gear were chatting and laughing with spectators, and presently I saw Roger, still wearing the blue and white scarf that matched the team strip, talking with several other spectators and a couple of players and, by their gestures, discussing the fortunes of the game.

Roger wasn't giving the conversation his full attention, but every now and then turning his head to look around, and it didn't require any psychic powers to guess who he was looking for. But there was no sign of Brent, and as everyone began to leave it became clear that he had left already.

I drove away, wishing I had never taken it on myself to push Roger toward going to the soccer. Certainly it hadn't brought about even the faintest dawn of a healing between them. I shook my head angrily. Who did I think I was, pontificating on other people's problems and relationships – even just in my own thoughts – when my own life was a tangle I couldn't begin to unravel?

As if to add another frustration to my list, my left front tyre picked up a nail and did what tyres normally do in the circumstances. I was in a side street where no knight in shining armour was likely to come by in the guise of a passing motorist offering assistance, but I wasn't unduly concerned at the prospect of changing a wheel. However, the wheel-nuts were stubborn and the daylight almost gone, and by the time I had completed the wheel-change it was virtually dark, and I was dirty and cold and distinctly irritable.

Had I not been, I might not even have particularly

registered the sound of breaking glass.

It was a non-residential part of the town, given over to light industry and commercial buildings – a car dealer, a garage, a small engineering works and similar things, I knew – all closed for the weekend. I remembered there was a shop specializing in audio and video equipment, and at once realized that what I'd heard in this empty street which wasn't particularly flush with lighting, was very probably a break-in.

Consequently the only intelligent thing to do was to get into my car and drive off to the police station, wherever it was, and report I'd heard suspicious sounds. I was still in too much of a filthy mood to feel, as I normally would, considerable relief that I'd finished the tyre-change and my car was mobile again, because no doubt whoever had just smashed a window thought he was alone in the street and might not be kindly disposed toward anyone who saw him. I started the car and flicked on the headlights, and saw my guess had been wrong: the window-breaker was not doing over the Hi-Fi and Television shop.

I hadn't realized I was so close to my father's plumbing business, but although it fronted another street, as I turned on the lights they shone directly across an open area where an old building had just been demolished, and on to the back of the workshop. A track-suited figure was standing there and, seemingly unaware of the fact that the headlights had picked him out, he picked up something from the ground and hurled it shatteringly through another window.

Even without the blue and white scarf around his neck I think I would have known who it was. Without stopping to think, I switched off the motor and, leaving the headlights on to light my way, I ran across the vacant lot. He was so totally, blindly intent on what he was doing that the sound of my footsteps blundering across the uneven ground didn't even register. He had a carpenter's wrecking-bar in his hands and he was trying to jemmy the back door.

'Brent!' I panted. 'For God's sake, stop!'

He wheeled around then, blinking a little in the glare of

the headlights. He was crying, his face twisted in rage, and I saw he was drunk. I saw also that at fifteen he was tough and muscular and much stronger than I was, and he held a deadly weapon in his hands if he translated that look of muderous hate into an almost reflex action at being disturbed. The realization that I had done something perhaps dangerously reckless jolted chillingly through me.

'It's all right, Brent,' I said quietly, trying desperately to sound as calm as I most emphatically was not. 'It's Lyn. I'm on your side, remember.'

'Get out,' he snarled. 'Get out and leave me alone.'

He wasn't going to use the wrecking-bar on me, I thought, or he'd have done it at once. A whisker of my original bravado came back.

'Give me that thing and come home with me to my place and let's sort this out.' I held out my hand for the bar.

He stepped back. 'I'm not going anywhere! Especially not with you.'

'Please yourself. But either you come with me or you go with the police.'

'Oh, so you're going to run to the cops, are you? Tell them some naughty boy's breaking up Daddy's shop?'

'Of course not. But they'll come, anyway. The racket you're making can be heard half a kilometre away.' I felt a bit of exaggeration did no harm. 'I suggest we get out of here before they turn up.'

He hesitated uncertainly and I pressed home my slight advantage. 'Come *on*, you clod! If you want to be tossed into clink for breaking and entering, I'm dashed if I want to be tossed in as an accessory. Let's go!'

I grabbed the wrecking-bar and his arm and steered him hurriedly back to the car, suddenly unresisting. I felt uneasily that we were shockingly obvious, picked out as we were by the headlights of my car as we blundered back across the demolition site. My desire not to be confronted by a patrolling police car was perfectly genuine and I was profoundly relieved when I had pushed a slightly unsteady Brent into the car and driven off to mingle anonymously with traffic in the main street, and no flashing blue lights or wailing sirens had accosted me.

We drove in silence for a while. I couldn't tell how much
of Brent's irrational behaviour was sheer, hurting anger,
and how much was alcohol. I guessed he was quite
unaccustomed to liquor and so probably had not drunk
very much before it tipped him over the edge of common
sense and into unthinking stupidity. I glanced at him. He
was staring straight ahead as if trying to come to grips with
what was happening.

Presently he said contemptuously, 'You're going the
wrong way.'

'Oh?' I said mildly. 'Well, I don't know this town all that
well. I thought it was the right way.'

'Where are you taking me?' There was just a hint of
alarm.

'I told you I'd take you home to my place. You can sleep
on the sofa overnight and I'll take you home in the
morning when you're fit to be seen.'

'They – Mum will be wondering where I am.'

'I'll phone her.'

'What'll you tell her?' The belligerence had faded a good
deal as some foggy degree of realization of his situation
sank in.

What indeed could I tell her? 'Some kind of a cover-up
story,' I said curtly. 'And I don't like being put in this kind
of situation.'

'Then you should have kept your beak out of it.'

I pulled the car over to the side of the road. 'If you want
to go back and finish what you were doing, feel free. I
don't know about you, but I think your mother is a very
nice lady, and I think she can do without any more
trouble.'

He put his hand on the door-catch and I thought, dear
Heaven, what do I do if he goes back?

Then he slumped back in his seat. 'Think you're smart,
don't you?' he muttered.

'Uh-huh,' I agreed cheerfully, and drove on, wishing I
could pretend to myself that the palms of my hands
weren't sweating.

Liam was sitting in his car outside the cottage when I pulled up, and my heart did a peculiar lurch, stirred by my mixed feelings of joy at seeing him and a desperate wish that he wasn't there to both witness and complicate this situation.

Brent sat upright at the sight of him. 'You called the cops!' he flung at me accusingly.

'Oh, sure,' I said. 'With my super-secret mental telepathy machine, I suppose? When did I have the chance to call the cops, you twit? Mr Stuart is friend of mine.'

Liam was watching alertly. I got out of the car and kissed him lightly.

'My passenger has been celebrating a day at soccer rather unwisely. It would upset his mother dreadfully if she saw him like this, so I'll spin her a good yarn and keep him here overnight till he sobers up. His mother's a friend of mine. I'm not sure how good he is at walking.'

I was unlocking the front door of the cottage as I spoke, and Liam opened the car door for Brent and took him by the arm. 'Come on, young feller,' he said easily, as if he were perfectly accustomed to his girl-friends bringing home drunken teenagers.

'Keep your hands off me!' Brent fumed. 'I can walk, let me tell you.' He turned on me. 'She's bloody well your stepmother. You thought about that? You're so smart. That makes me your stepbrother. You thought about that? You're so –'

He had been on his feet unsteadily, holding the car door, the numbing effect of alcohol seemingly growing worse. I was never quite sure whether he simply lost his balance as he tried to walk, or whether he had some assistance from Liam, but I suspect the latter. Whatever the cause he pitched forward and sprawled face down on the gravel path. Liam hauled him to his feet unceremoniously.

'Keep your –' Brent began and then gave a gasp of pain. 'You're hurting my arm, you –'

'Good,' Liam said calmly. 'And if you so much as open your mouth again I'll hurt it a great deal more. Now you will walk indoors; you will take a shower; and you will sleep wherever this lady is kind enough to give you a bed. You will thank your lucky stars she found you, and in the morning when you're sober enough you will apologize for all the trouble you've caused. You hear me?'

'I am her stepbrother,' Brent muttered insistently while I felt coldly sick.

'Some people have all the luck.' Liam pushed him into the bathroom. 'Shower.'

He shut the door and looked at me. 'Liam,' I began, and he interrupted as if he hadn't heard me.

'Are you really going to let him sleep here?'

'I can't let his mother see him like this.'

'Maybe she's used to it.'

I shook my head. 'I don't think so.'

'All right. You phone her and I'll make up a bed for his highness in the spare room. What's his name, by the way?'

'Brent. Brent Watson.'

He nodded and went off to the little spare bedroom leaving me to the telephone. Sally answered at once and there was a note of anxiety in her voice.

'It's Lyn, Sally.' I did my best to sound cheerful. 'Look, I'm sure you're beginning to worry, but Brent's with me. I had a flat tyre on the way home, so I've just got back, and it seems Brent needs to talk about a few things. It's going to be late, so I've suggested he bunk down in the spare room for the night. I hope you don't mind.'

'Oh, Lyn, I hope he's not being a bother,' she said in a mixture of relief and uneasiness.

'Of course not. Please don't think I'm trying to play the amateur psychologist or anything. But maybe there really are things he and I can sort out – at least begin to. Do you mind? He seemed pretty upset.'

'Of course I don't mind. I was getting worried about him – he never skips a soccer match. I hope he doesn't upset you, that's all.'

'No, no, nothing like that,' I assured her.

He's only told Liam so much of who I am that I have to tell him the whole story now. I should have, anyway. And risk him walking out of my life.

I went into the kitchen and began to try to think about preparing a meal. What would happen when Roger discovered the damage to his workshop? Would he dismiss it as casual vandalism or, as there probably would be marks to indicate an attempt to jemmy the door open, would he call the police? On the whole I thought not. Roger Miller had his own reasons for not wanting to draw police attention to himself in any way. Would he suspect Brent? Should I try to persuade Brent to tell Roger what he'd done? No, I decided; I simply didn't know what was the best thing to do, so I had better leave that one alone.

I must have been standing irresolutely by the sink, vegetables on the draining-board waiting to be prepared, a good deal longer than I realized. I didn't even hear Liam come in until he put his arms around me.

'Well, Brent's flaked out completely. He did manage a shower and got his underpants on and I dumped him into bed like that. I'd take a bet he'll sleep till morning. I was planning to take you out to dinner, but just in case your house-guest does surface and sets the place on fire or something, we'd better not leave him alone.'

'I was just getting a meal ready.'

He kissed the top of my head. 'Leave it. You look as if you've had enough for one day. For quite a few days. Light the fire and pour yourself a drink while I go out and get us a takeaway dinner. Food to go, as the Americans call it. There's a good Chinese place where they do very tasty food. Do you eat Chinese?'

'That would be fine. Liam –' I swallowed.

He shook his head. 'Later.'

I had the fire going warmly when he came back. I'd checked on Brent and found him sleeping heavily, as Liam had said. He must have been much drunker than I'd realized, and only his frustration and rage had kept him mobile. I was both surprised and touched to see how carefully Liam had pulled the covers over him, and made sure he would be warm. Looking down at him, I wondered what he was really like, this boy who was my stepbrother and whom I had only seen consumed by anger and a sense of betrayal.

I knew that feeling, in a sense, since childhood. My own anger against Brent for his senseless attempt at some kind of revenge faded, and I hoped that in the morning he and I could talk freely – whether helpfully or not, goodness only knew.

Liam was right: the Chinese food he brought in was very good, though I had some difficulty eating. Somehow we managed a fairly easy conversation, and it was only when we were having coffee in front of the fire that I felt I had to explain Brent's comments.

'Thank you for taking charge of Brent for me,' I said. 'You took it in your stride as if you were accustomed to handling young fools who'd gone out and got themselves drunk and disorderly.'

He smiled ruefully. 'I've handled a few.'

'Liam, he was right when he said he's my stepbrother. But his stepfather is my father, Roger Miller. Only –'

'Only his real name is Roger Sutton and he did a long stretch for robbery and murder.'

As I stared at him, stunned, he put his coffee mug down and reached across to take my hand. 'It's all right, Lyn. I know who you are. I've always known, since that afternoon on the roadside when you told me your name.'

'You've *known*?' Total bewilderment must have shown in my voice. 'But – how? It's nearly twenty years, and by comparison with other crimes it wasn't especially sensational. No one would remember now, except the people involved. Why do you know about us – Roger and me?'

'Because of my job. I haven't levelled with you, Lyn, because I've been afraid I'd lose you if you knew. Silly, of course, because eventually you'd have had to know. I've just gone on delaying telling you.'

I shook my head as if to try to clear my brain. It was like being in a play that had gone wrong, hearing another actor speaking my lines.

'I don't understand,' I said numbly.

'I told you I had a public service job. That's true, partly, but sometimes a half-truth is no better than a lie. I'm a policeman.'

I think I understood a moment before he actually spoke the words. A policeman. Dear God. A policeman didn't marry into the family of a convicted major criminal – a killer – especially when the bulk of the loot from his crime was still unaccounted for. There was no doubt I had a fantastic talent for choosing men. First a lawyer who couldn't hamper his career with a crim's daughter, and now a policeman whose career I would hardly enhance either.

'If I'd told you,' Liam said, 'you'd think I was only here to spy on your father – maybe even that I was spying on you. And that would be the end of it. You wouldn't want to know me. I guess that *is* the way of it.'

There was a silence while I slowly focussed my thoughts: Liam was telling me he was afraid *I* wouldn't want *him* in my life.

'You're speaking my lines,' I finally managed to say.

'What?'

'That day by the river, when you showed me the place to paint, you asked if there was a man in my life and I told you he went to Western Australia and lost my address. He did both those things when I told him about my father. I've been afraid to tell you for fear you'd follow him. Now it's even worse than I thought. He was a bright young lawyer. I didn't belong in his life, damaging his career. You're a policeman. An ex-con's daughter doesn't belong in your life either.'

'Any more than a cop belongs in yours? Is that what you're saying?'

'That's nonsense!'

'And I am not about to go to Western Australia and lose your address.'

I'm not quite sure just how we got into each other's arms, but it was quite some time before we came to be sitting quietly in front of the fire again. Liam carefully coaxed it back to crackling life and we sat on the hearth-rug with my head against his shoulder.

'We haven't solved anything,' I said.

He grinned. 'I thought we'd done rather well.'

'Don't dodge the issue. There's an awful lot I still don't understand. About why you're here, and how you know so much about my father. You're not a Queensland policeman – what's your rank, by the way?'

'Detective Senior Sergeant,' he said quietly.

'My father's crime was committed in Queensland, and long before you joined the force. He was convicted, he served his sentence. I believe he's gone straight since?'

'As far as I'm aware, yes. Sure.'

'The only thing of any possible interest to anyone is the fact of the missing jewels, and I'm not sure they'd be of official police interest in Queensland, let alone interstate. And sadly there are plenty of totally unsolved crimes, some of an even worse nature, to occupy official minds and time. Why the interest in Roger Sutton-cum-Miller?

'I'm not here to spy on your father, Lyn. My interest in him isn't even really official, though quite a lot of money was involved in the disappearance of the contents of that jewellery store, and I gather it rankled with the Queensland chaps, and a thing like that is never entirely forgotten. But I got interested through an uncle who was with the insurance company that had written the cover for the jewellery. The company paid up, of course, long ago. But my uncle never could get the thing out of his mind, and even after all those years, afterwards, when I went into the force, he told me about it, and he has never really left it alone. He kept track of Roger Sutton – knew when he was released; what he did afterwards; knew he'd changed his name, remarried, lived here, had his own business, kept his hands clean – the lot. He always kept me posted, as it were. "Something's wrong," he has said to me more than once. "Sutton should have capitalized on those stones long before this. I can understand he'd have the sense not to move on them as soon as he got out, but in all the years since then he hasn't shown any sign of suddenly coming into money. He's up to something, but I'm damned if I know what." '

Liam turned his head to look at me. 'I'm sorry. I shouldn't talk to you like this. He's your father.'

'It's all right,' I said urgently. 'Go on. I want to know all there is to know, and Roger won't tell me. Not everything, anyway.'

'Well, you see, my uncle was the fellow actually responsible for accepting the insurance risk on that jewellery store, and his company hierarchy were not wildly impressed when they found the place could so readily be burgled and the alarm system bypassed. Uncle Joe felt it damaged his career considerably, and he always wanted to get to the bottom of it. It's always been a very personal thing with him. He asked me to get our chaps here to keep an eye on Roger Miller with a view to noting any apparent sudden acquistion of wealth.'

He hesitated. 'My uncle is totally convinced Roger Miller knows where the missing stuff is, and one day he won't be able to resist the temptation to go and get it. And if that happens, Uncle Joseph badly wants to know. I'd never seen your father until I came here on sick leave.'

'But your friend Glen Harlin has been keeping an eye on him.'

'Lyn —'

'I know. It's part of your job. It's all right. I know you have to do it.' I looked at the fire for a minute or so. 'But suppose everyone has been wrong. Suppose Roger always told the truth: someone else was there before him?'

He didn't answer immediately. 'Do you believe that?'

I took a long breath. 'I don't know. That's the worst part, I think. Roger says if he admitted the whole thing everyone would believe him, but when he denies it they don't know whether to believe him or not. He's right.'

'That's what's wrong with Brent, I suppose?'

I nodded. 'Roger hadn't told them. Then I came along and everything came out. I only wanted to get to know my father and make my own judgment of the sort of man he really is, whether he was guilty as charged or not. But I've only hurt everyone.'

He laid a hand gently against my cheek. 'Not everyone.'

We sat in silence for a while and then I said, 'Liam, you said once that you might have to go back to farming. I took it then that you meant you might have to be invalided out of – well, your public service job – because of your accident. I didn't understand at the time why farming would be easier than the public service. Maybe I do now. Was it in fact because you felt that with me in your life – a murderer's daughter at worst, a thief's daughter at best – you couldn't stay in the police force?'

'Not because of you.' He shook his head. 'Not because of any accident.'

He stood up, pulled off his sweater, unbuttoned his shirt. 'I didn't actually say I'd been in an accident – just that I'd got knocked about. I let you think it was a motorcycle accident because I didn't want to tell you I was a cop.' He had his shirt off now. 'You asked if I was the only one hurt in my accident and I told you someone was killed. I promised I'd tell you one day – I knew I'd have to. Look closely at these scars now that you know what I am.'

Puzzled, I studied the obvious surgical scars that slashed across his upper abdomen and ran around his rib cage. He turned to let me see his back. Then he put his shirt back on. 'Any idea what sort of surgery that was?' There was strain in his voice, a kind of tension, almost harshness.

'Well,' I hedged, 'I can see, of course, that the scars aren't very old, but I know that anyway. My knowledge of anatomy isn't all that good, and surgical procedures are pretty much a closed book, but I'd say maybe you'd had your spleen removed and perhaps there'd been some lung –'

I stopped, suddenly understanding. 'Oh, God,' I whispered. 'You were shot.'

He was pulling his sweater on over his head. 'Right,' was all he said.

He sat down again. 'Liam,' I said very quietly, 'it must have been –'

'Close?' The harshness of stress was still in his voice. 'Yes. At the time I felt it hadn't been close enough. I wondered why he couldn't have finished *me* instead of her.'

'Her,' I said gently. 'Do you want to tell me? Don't feel you must.'

He shook his head. 'I guess I need to tell you.' He spread his hands and looked at them, his eyes heavy with the memory.

'It was that old, old time-bomb, the domestic situation gone violent. Fellow killed his wife. Neighbours heard shots and called police. A patrol car turned up, and as the fellows got out a couple of shots flattened a front tyre and smashed a radiator and the guy started yelling that he was holed up in the house with his six-year-old daughter and if anyone tried to come in he'd kill her too.

'I was among the reinforcements who went to the scene. It was a long day and a long night. We kept the place surrounded, as unobtrusively as possible. We had the man's relatives there to try to talk to him on the phone. We had an ambulance. We had a psychiatrist. Everyone trying to persuade him to let the little girl go. In fact we didn't even know whether she was alive or not. He said his wife was dead, and by and large we believed him, though we couldn't be sure of that, either. He stayed awake, right through, and he made sure we knew it. Every now and then he'd fire another shot at random, just to make sure we kept our heads down, I guess.

'By morning his relatives – father and sister – said his telephone conversations were becoming incoherent. He wouldn't talk to anyone but them, so the psychiatrist was hampered. The general conclusion was that the subject would eventually fall asleep from exhaustion and then maybe we could quietly close on him. We thought perhaps his incoherent talk was the onset of exhaustion, but the psychiatrist warned that, whether exhaustion or not, the confusion might well indicate he was more dangerous, more unpredictable.'

He paused and swallowed hard, and beads of sweat stood out on his face, remembering.

'The psychiatrist had just finished telling us that, and I picked up my bullet-proof vest to put it on in case things suddenly began to happen, and the marksmen began to ready themselves for God only knew what. The front door was flung open without warning and a little blonde-haired girl was pushed out. She was dressed in pyjamas – blue, with little white rabbits – and she was holding a battered old teddy-bear. I remember – remember the tremendous surge of relief I felt. I guess we all felt the same.

'Her father yelled at her: "Run! Go on! Run!" And she did. She ran towards us and her grandfather called "Sandy, Sandy!" And her father shot her. He kept shooting from the doorway. I raced in towards the little girl where she lay in the driveway, and he shot me too.

'Only difference was, when our riflemen finally caught a glimpse of enough of him to put a bullet through his arm and let the ambulance people get to us, I was still breathing and she wasn't.'

He put his hands over his face as if in a desperately futile effort to shut out the scene, and I put my arms around him and suddenly he was crying, shaking with racking sobs. I just went on holding him, remembering that Sally Miller had said my father cried out in his sleep: 'He's dead! My God, he's dead!' These two men who shared my life from such different angles were haunted by the same kind of nightmare.

Presently Liam was no longer shaken by sobbing. He wiped his face and held me gently close against him for a moment. 'So much for the big tough policeman,' he said wryly. 'Sorry, Lyn.'

'Sorry for what? Being human?' I smiled at him. 'I think maybe you should have done that a long time ago.' I touched his cheek. 'Liam, none of it was your fault. Everything that could have been done, was done. However awful, none of it was your fault. None of it was anyone's fault, except her father's. You must hold on to that. He was to blame, and only he.'

He nodded. 'I know. That's what the psychiatrist said when I was in hospital. That's what he told all the cops involved. That slime never intended to let the little girl go. He just didn't have the guts to shoot her face to face.'

'What – happened to him?'

'He managed to turn the gun on himself, in spite of a bullet through one arm. He made a good job of it. I rather doubt any of our chaps would have been trying very hard to stop him.'

After a little silence Liam said, 'That's what I was thinking of when I said I might have to go back to farming. Every cop has to understand that some day, somewhere, maybe tomorrow, maybe not for twenty years, he may very well be confronted with an armed ratbag. He has to be confident he can face up to it. His colleagues have to be confident he can face up to it along with them and not crack. If ever I'm faced with something like that again, I'm going to see a little girl in blue pyjamas running to what she thought was safety. I'm not sure, not by a long way, that I can handle it. You saw me just now. Whenever I think of it my hands shake and I break out in a sweat. I might have to make very fast, logical assessments of such a situation again, one day. Lives might depend on it – depend on a cop who won't fall apart under the pressure. All my life I'll be left to think that if I'd ordered our marksmen to open up on the house the moment that little kid came out of the door – if we'd laid down a covering fire – he might not have got his shots home. She might have lived. I should have used my pistol and blazed away at the door, or shown myself earlier and drawn his fire.'

'You had no time.'

He gave me a quick hug and smiled. 'Thanks. Thanks for making excuses for me.'

'I'm not making excuses; I'm pointing out facts.'

He sighed. 'The simple fact is I don't know whether I can ever again be a good cop. Or whether I even want to be. Or whether I'm reduced to being a gutless wonder whenever the chips are down. That's the real reason I'm on extended sick leave – not so much the physical damage. That will heal with time.'

'So will the emotional damage. There'll be scars there, too, I guess, and they'll affect the way you think, but they won't cripple you, Liam. I'm sure of that.'

'I love you,' he said softly. 'Don't you *mind* me being a

cop?'

'I want you to be what *you* want to be. I'll accept it, whatever you decide, one hundred per cent. If you'll have me.'

'I'll have you,' he said, and his voice wasn't entirely steady.

We just went on sitting in front of the fire, my hand in his, silently and at peace with ourselves. I thought then of an old poem I'd heard somewhere: *The grace to live in a world at war, and still maintain the heart's own private peace.* That was what Liam and I had together, our own sanctuary where we could retreat from whatever private wars were raging around us; where we could regroup our thoughts and hopes and strengths to go out and deal with the outside world again. We were incredibly lucky people.

After a while Liam said, 'How did you come to find Brent this evening?'

'I'd been changing a tyre in one of the side streets and I heard glass breaking. He was smashing up his stepfather's workshop. He'd only just started, thank goodness. Broke a couple of windows and was trying to force the door. I shudder to think of the trail of damage if he'd got inside. He was so drunk he could hardly stand up, as you saw. I think only a kind of fury was keeping him going.'

'What are you going to do?'

'I told his mother he'd come here to talk and as it would be late I'd suggested he bunk down for the night. She was happy to accept that. I'm hoping Roger will accept the inference that damage to the shop was by unknown vandals. I hope he doesn't even bother to report it to the police. Is that very bad of me?'

He grinned. 'I'll just mention to Glen that if they do get a report, the best they can do is put it down to anonymous vandals and add it to the unsolved-crimes list.'

Nine

After a shower and coffee next morning it was a subdued Brent, sullen and pale with embarrassment and a hangover, who sat at my table, not looking at me.

'Did you play in your soccer match yesterday before you went off on a binge?' I asked conversationally.

'Yes.'

'Good. You didn't let your team down. Did you win?'

'Yes.'

'Great. What was the score?'

'Two-one.'

'Close. What position do you play?'

'Goalie. Listen, why don't you just get on with the lecture?'

'I don't know much about soccer, but I always think the goalie's job is the toughest and most vital of all, but they never seen to be the real glamour players. If a team wins, it's because the goalkeeper saved the other side's strikes from going home, isn't it?'

He looked at me doubtfully. 'It's because of a lot of things, not just the goalkeeper.'

'I guess you're right. If a team wins, it's because of the whole team, and every member won, not just those who scored. If a family hangs together it wins, too, and every member wins. Don't let your home team down, Brent. I know you wanted to hurt Roger, but you'd have hurt everybody – yourself, Rosemary, especially your mother. If the team loses, every member loses, not just the goalkeeper who missed the ball or the striker who missed the net. OK, end of lecture. I'll drive you home.'

He followed me out to the car in silence, and as I started the motor I said, 'If anyone remarks that you look a bit pale, we had a Chinese meal last night and you might have over-eaten. I told your mother you'd come over to talk, and as I was so late home I'd suggested you bunk down here, because it was going to be pretty late when we finished talking.'

'Thanks,' he said reluctantly. 'The shop –'

'A couple of broken windows will be put down to unknown vandals, I'm sure.'

He didn't say anything more on the way home. I talked about sport I'd played, any absurdities of victory or loss I could recall, and generally avoided seriousness or any hint of further lecturing. Once I said casually, 'Roger went to watch the soccer yesterday. He'll be pleased you won.'

Brent turned his head to flick a surprised glance at me, but said nothing. I stopped the car not quite outside the Miller house. I didn't particularly want to see anyone and have to weave any more fabrications. As Brent got out of the car I picked the wrecking-bar he'd been using yesterday off the floor of the car.

'Better put this back,' I said.

Our eyes met for a moment and I smiled at him. 'See you later, Brent.' I raised a hand in farewell.

'Yeah. See you.' He hesitated, looked down at the wrecking-bar in his hand and then back at me, and suddenly he smiled. 'Thanks, Lyn. You're all right.' And he turned and walked away.

You're all right. That's what Edith Wishart had said. And now I had to attend her funeral, and begin the wondering all over again.

Liam's Uncle Joseph of the insurance company believed my father was 'up to something.' Was someone in the Norris household up to something also, or was that person now forever removed?

More people than I had expected attended the funeral, an Anglican service, kept simple and dignified. The words were almost a blur in my mind – the analogy of the grass which flourishes in the morning and in the evening it is cut down. I had talked to Edith Wishart in the morning, and she had wanted to tell me something; and in the evening she had been cut down indeed; and whether by accident, her own hand, or someone else's, we might never know.

Vi and Ivan were there, of course, and Peter, white-faced in his wheelchair with Arnold Bright walking beside; otherwise there were mostly older people, and I recalled that Edith had lived here much longer than Ivan and Vi, and would have had her own friends. Glen Harlin was there with another man and I felt a sense of shock for a moment. The police presence, unobtrusive as it was in ordinary business suits, seemed to me a clear statement to all and sundry that the accident or suicide theory was not totally accepted. And it occurred to me, as Glen Harlin met my eyes briefly and nodded recognition, that the statement was being deliberately made.

Possibly, too, the detectives wanted to observe the mourners. Just as I did.

Mourners. Was there someone there who was not mourning in the least? Not among her elderly friends, several of them visibly grieving. Ivan and Vi were grave but composed, as one would expect. After all, Edith had been an aunt by marriage only; and, although evidently she had been to a fair extent their benefactor, there had not seemed to me a very close affection between them. They could be expected to be saddened, and somewhat distressed by the nature of her death, but not distraught.

Peter, on the other hand, looked like someone who had suffered a severe shock. Pale, with dark circles of sleeplessness under his eyes, his hands gripped whitely on the arms of his chair. I remembered Edith Wishart's concern for him the day the car ran down through the garden. Hard to imagine that was only a handful of days ago. She had said that Peter often used to visit her, but didn't do so any more, and obviously that saddened her. She had been fond of Peter. Had he been fond of her? He must have been, once, when he often visited her. Why had he stopped going to see her? And when?

As people filed out at the conclusion of the service, Peter looked at me for a moment, a look of burning intensity as if he wanted to read my thoughts. I wished I could interpret that look. Arnold Bright, following Peter, was watching him with a concerned expression.

I stood outside in the sun of a beautiful day, surprisingly mild for this time of year as late autumn slid into winter, and for a moment I watched fallen liquidamber leaves scuffled by a little breeze, and I thought of death and life and realized I felt very real sadness over Edith Wishart. In the very brief time I'd known her, I had come to like her. Perhaps a good deal of my sadness was at the thought that a sharp mind had let itself creep down into dependency on alcohol that blurred it. A *waste*. I didn't like waste. And Peter's dependency on his wheelchair – not any fault of his own – what a waste of his talents.

Ivan was beside me, saying, 'Lyn, will you come out to the house when we leave the cemetery? We're asking people to come out for a light lunch – some have travelled a bit of a distance, probably. We'd like you to come, and I'm sure it would help Peter. We greatly appreciate the fact that you came to the service.'

He smiled courteously and was gone to speak to others without waiting for me to answer.

I followed the little straggling procession of cars out to the Norris house where Vi had set out a buffet lunch of cold meat and salad and bread rolls, and people helped themselves and chatted to people they knew. The detectives had not come – doubtless they had not been asked. Ivan introduced me to a couple of people who had been friends of Edith's, but after the exchange of a few sober pleasantries I felt I wanted to be alone and went out on to the verandah to look at the scene I had tried to capture with oil paints. One never did, really, I thought, looking at it. Nothing ever came near the reality. But the painting was finished now and while I was never actually satisfied with my work, I wasn't entirely displeased with it, either.

Vi came out on the verandah to offer me a drink and

urge me to help myself to more food. 'How is the painting coming along?' she asked.

'I've finished it. I'll bring it out to let you see it.'

'Oh, yes, please.' She smiled at me. 'We'd like that very much. If you could, though, would you come out some time in the next few days? Not tomorrow, there are legal things to attend to. But we're going away for a while at the end of the week – a couple of weeks up north in the Whitsunday Islands and the Barrier Reef. It will be good for all of us to get away for a while, after this sad business – especially Peter. He's really quite badly upset, I'm afraid, though he doesn't talk about it.'

'He must have been quite fond of Mrs Wishart,' I said.

'Yes.' She looked a shade doubtful. 'They used to get on very well, but – well, I suppose Peter has always been different since his accident. But Aunt Edith's death has no doubt brought back memories of losing his mother. If we get him away for a while – up into that good Queensland winter sun – I think it will help a lot.'

'I'm sure it will,' I said warmly. 'The Whitsundays are lovely, and it's easy to take trips to the reef, and there'll be lots of things for Peter to do, even though he can't walk. I think it's a great idea.'

'Perhaps if you know the area a bit you could talk to Peter about it,' Vi suggested. 'We can't seem to get him really interested in going.'

'Of course,' I agreed, and Vi excused herself and returned to her other guests. I turned back to the view and saw Peter sitting in his wheelchair on the concrete path at the end of the verandah, watching me.

'Hello.' I walked over to him. 'You must be very sad, Peter. I'm sorry. I liked Mrs Wishart a lot.'

He looked at me in that strange way he had done in the Church – almost a *calculating* look. 'Yes,' he said, turning his head away. 'She taught me to play backgammon,' he added, as if that explained a lot. In a way, I felt it did.

'She was going to teach me, too,' I told him. Then, after a pause, 'Vi was just telling me you're all going up to the Whitsunday Islands for a holiday. You'll love it, I'm sure.

It's beautiful there. And if you go on to one of the other islands, one of the coral cays right on the reef itself, like Heron Island, you'll be able to go out in a glass-bottomed boat to look down at the coral. And the fish —'

'I've seen pictures.' His interruption was not meant to be discourteous, I was sure. It was rather a plea to be left alone.

Curious, I asked, 'Don't you want to go?'

He shrugged and, not looking at me, said flatly, 'It doesn't make any difference.' And he wheeled quickly away.

'He's very upset,' Arnold Bright said behind me. He was watching the retreating form in the wheelchair with a concerned, almost troubled, expression. I liked the quietly-spoken teacher with his serious grey eyes and his concern for the boy whose accident he felt was partially his fault for simply assuming the climbing-ropes were in the undamaged condition it had been reasonable to expect. No doubt there was one simple truth for every occupation where any degree of risk arose — from law-enforcement and medicine to abseiling: never take anything for granted.

'Peter must have been very fond of Mrs Wishart,' I said, wondering how many times I'd already said that today.

Arnold nodded. 'Before his accident he often used to go to her flat and they'd play board games and he liked to have her tell him stories about past times around the district — especially stories about the Bartholomews — the family after whom the mountain was named and who tried to farm there for three generations till poor country and finally a fire sent them bankrupt.'

He smiled. 'In fact, I'm inclined to think she made up some of the stories for Peter's entertainment, and I think he maybe suspected it, too, but he loved to hear. He loves that place out there where that old shed is all that's left. He always used to call it *his* place, and say that one day when he'd made enough money as a wildlife photographer he'd buy it and build a house there.' He shook his head. 'You'd think he'd hate it now, because it was on the cliff there that he fell. But he still likes me to take him out there. Sometimes I take him for a picnic lunch there, and for a while a bit of the old Peter shows through.'

He made an apologetic little gesture. 'Sorry. I tend to go rattling on.'

That was not something I'd ever have accused Arnold Bright of doing. I said, 'Everyone says how different Peter is since his accident. I think, that day when he showed me some of his photographs, I caught a glimpse of what he used to be like.'

Arnold nodded. 'He was just a lively, normal kid – actually very mature for his years, but with a great sense of fun and an extraordinary talent, as you saw in the photographs.'

'Yes. Of course, to have your mobility and your dream of a career smashed in a couple of seconds is a massive trauma. It wouldn't be reasonable to expect the emotional injuries to have done too much healing in a year.'

'No, certainly not. But I'd have thought, given Peter's personality, that he wouldn't be quite the way he is. It's as though –'

He stopped as abruptly as if someone had hit him and I looked at him. He was staring blankly into the distance and for a moment I thought he'd been taken ill.

'Oh, my God,' he said very softly. 'I wonder if I've been a blind fool.'

He turned to me, his eyes intent. 'Do we know who Peter is?' he demanded.

'Well, he's the son of some sort of cousin of Vi's, as I –'

'I don't mean that,' he said impatiently. 'Do we know who he *is*?'

'I'm sorry,' I said stupidly. 'I don't think I understand.'

'No, of course.' He managed a courteous smile but it was clearly designed to cover what he felt had been an indiscretion. 'I'm sorry. I was talking in nonsensical riddles.' He glanced back into the fairly crowded house and added, 'There's Ivan. I must just have a word with him. Will you excuse me?'

He nodded politely and slipped into the living-room, but

he didn't go near Ivan or stop to speak to anyone. Unobtrusively but purposefully he went straight through the room and out a side door and a few seconds later I saw his car swing out into the drive and go off down the road, not hurrying, still keeping a low profile as if not wanting anyone who happened to notice to give it a second thought.

Damn it, I thought, suddenly angry; wouldn't *anyone* in this place take me into their confidence? Arnold had felt suddenly and awkwardly that he had said too much of whatever he was thinking. Why? What was he thinking that I was not trusted to know about?

I sighed. It brought me back to my own problem of wrestling with a question of whether or not to take someone into my confidence.

I badly wanted to tell Liam about Vi – show him the note he had delivered on her behalf, and find out what he thought of the whole thing. After all, he was trained to deal with people who rightly or wrongly felt their lives were threatened. I had wanted to tell him before I knew he was a policeman. Now I wanted his advice even more. But – he was a policeman. He would see the situation through a policeman's eyes. And that was exactly what Vi had begged Lillian not to allow to happen. She believed that the line the police would take would greatly increase her peril.

Did that peril still exist – if it ever had existed? Or had Edith Wishart's death eliminated the perceived danger, whether Vi's fears were justified or not? I felt reasonably sure those fears had been the product of some temporary, though possibly recurring, phobia which now seemed blanked out of her memory. That seemed the logical explanation. But phobia or not, fear could drive a person to kill, and there were strange circumstances in Edith's death. If there was even the slightest chance Vi had stepped over the edge of sanity, what right had I to hide what I knew? How well did I know anyone connected with this household? I needed more time before I could make a decision.

The only thing I could feel reasonably confident about

was that Vi was not afraid of Ivan. She might feel he would never believe her fears for her life were justified, but I was sure he was not the basis of those fears.

I looked around the garden for Peter, but predictably there was no sign of him, so I made quiet farewells of Ivan and Vi, with their reminders that I must bring the painting out for them to see. I drove away, thinking about my relationship with them. In the weeks since I had first come here they had been cordial, welcoming, showing every sign of friendship, seeming to *want* to be friends. Yet we were not really friends at all. Even though I may have saved Vi from serious injury and possibly death, and that necessarily established some sort of bond, there was none of the spontaneous warmth of real friendship. I reflected that at all levels of human relationships that warmth, that rapport, was something which just simply and sometimes inexplicably *happened*. It was said in truth that friendship could not be bought. It was equally true that it couldn't be *created*, even if both parties would have liked it to be so.

Meanwhile, the Norrises and I would have to settle for a pleasant, amicable acquaintance. Sometimes from that, real friendships grew.

Dinner at the home of Glen and Julie Harlin, on the other hand, did have that immediately comfortable air of easy comradeship, from jokes about Julie's cooking – led by Julie herself – to Glen raising his glass to me and saying smilingly, 'We've been worried about what sort of girl would be silly enough to take on young Liam here, but bless me if he hasn't gone and found one who isn't silly at all. He's a lucky feller, Lyn.'

The conversation came to questions about my painting, and I told how I had met Peter Fisher. 'There,' I said, 'is talent far beyond mine, even though it is in a different field. And it's lost. It's a tragedy. There are many things that can be achieved by people in wheelchairs, but being a world-class wildlife photographer isn't one of them.'

We talked about it for a few minutes and I got the snapshot of Peter from my purse and showed it to them.

'That's Peter as he was,' I said. 'Peter as he should be.'

Liam sat looking at the photograph for a long moment, his face suddenly stonily blank. Finally he roused himself and handed it back.

'There are many ways of being crippled,' he said, and a strange little chill fell on me.

Perhaps the others felt it also, because there was a moment's silence before Julie said, 'Your Peter looks to me like a great kid. I'll bet he'll make his mark in the world at something, even if it's not what he planned. Do you know the other day I saw a photograph of a blind man playing golf? Golf! I can't hit the dashed ball when I can *see* it. Do you play, Lyn?'

And the conversation became easy and comfortable again.

After the meal, which was quite excellent in spite of the good-natured jokes, I told the men to talk shop or fishing, whichever they fancied, while I helped Julie clear away.

Naturally enough, no one had said anything about my relationship to Roger Miller, but I wanted a police-wife's opinion on what effect it would have on Liam's career, and after only a few hours' acquaintance I felt comfortable enough with Julie to ask.

She was stacking dishes at the sink when I asked, and she went very still for a moment before she turned to look at me, her attractive face serious and thoughtful.

'I don't think Liam will stay in the force,' she said quietly. 'But it's not because of you and your father.'

'He told me he was afraid he'd not be able to handle it if he ever had to face a gunman again. He told me – about the little girl.'

'I'm glad he talked about it.' Julie sounded relieved. 'He wouldn't, for a long time. He's been keeping it all locked up inside, festering in his mind. But even before that happened he had thoughts of leaving the force. I don't know how serious he was about it, but I think it was something he was really considering. The family still own a farm somewhere, I believe, and Liam has considered going back to manage it himself instead of employing someone as they do now. But I think – and so does Glen – that he hates the thought of quitting police work because of being afraid of not handling it when the chips are down.'

She added quickly, 'He's no coward, Lyn. Don't think that. He's got what Glen calls golden guts. He ran out, that day, into a steady stream of gunshots. And it's not the first time he's faced a madman, or a gun, or both. The thing is, if he stays with the police, he'll very likely face the same sort of situation again. I don't think he's afraid he can't face a bullet himself. But he *is* afraid his judgment will always be clouded by what happened to that little girl – and himself – and he might find he can't make quick decisions because of that.'

'And if he leaves the force people will think he's a coward. And, worse, he may think so himself,' I added.

Julie nodded. 'That's why he's on extended leave. Physically he's probably almost well enough to resume normal duties, but he still needs time to get himself sorted out. He could go back to a desk job, but I don't think he considers that an option. It's terribly important that if he leaves the force it's because he wants to – not because he has to. He's had professional counselling, of course, but I guess in the end it's up to him. And,' she added with a smile, 'now he's met you, and believe me, it's doing him more good than any amount of psychiatric help. He loves you, Lyn. Very much.'

'It's mutual,' I said. Then, 'You haven't answered my question: if Liam stays in the force, how much damage would a wife like me do to his career?'

'I should think a wife like you would be a tremendous help to him in any career.'

'You're dodging the issue. Let me put it more bluntly: if he's married to a murderer's daughter, his chances of promotion are going to be affected, aren't they? The powers that be will have to take into account the public perception of a high-ranking cop who married into a crim's family.'

Julie spread her hands in a gesture of helplessness. 'I simply don't know, Lyn. I've never encountered a situation like that. Or maybe I have, but it had been kept secret.'

'I wouldn't be involved in that – keeping my background

secret, I mean; and I'm sure Liam wouldn't, either. That's what I've done all my life, and it's an endless situation of living in fear that someone is going to find out. I've had enough of that. Though I wouldn't reveal that Roger Miller is Roger Sutton – that's his life and his decision, not mine.'

Julie nodded. 'Fair enough. Maybe, because of your father, Liam mightn't ever be made Commissioner, or even Chief Inspector, but I don't need to tell you the obvious fact that an awful lot of career policemen don't go that high and are quite content not to. I can tell you one thing with absolute certainty: if Liam decides to stay in the force, you are more important to him than any promotional prospects. By a long way.'

Our eyes met and I saw the conviction in hers and I smiled. 'Thank you, Julie.'

There was a little silence while we dealt with the dishes and thought our own thoughts. Presently I said slowly, perhaps beginning to understand for the first time the almost sub-conscious fear every policeman's wife has to live with, 'I guess, in the end, Liam can't know whether he can handle a dangerous confrontation until he actually faces one again.'

And Julie, with a police-wife's knowledge that any day, any hour, her husband can be faced with just the kind of violence that haunted Liam, nodded.

Ten

It was as we were driving back to the cottage that evening that Liam told me he would be away the following day, and perhaps longer.

'A couple of things I have to see to,' he said. 'I'm not sure how long it'll take.'

I literally felt my stomach muscles jerk tight in a cold knot. It was too close in time to my conversation with Julie. It was too close to what Eric had said before he went across the continent and over the borders of my life.

I swallowed and said with an effort to be casual, 'Are you driving up to Sydney?'

He shook his head, unaware, apparently, of my sense of being threatened with a loss that seemed beyond enduring. 'No. I have to go to Melbourne, actually. I'm catching an early flight tomorrow morning. I'm not sure how long my business there will take, and I haven't asked about the return-flight schedule, so unless there's a flight leaving Melbourne pretty late, I should think I'll have to stay over at least one night.'

He grinned that schoolboy grin. 'Promise you'll miss me dreadfully.'

'I'll put a note on my fridge door reminding me to be devastated,' I said brightly. But I felt as cold as the inside of any refrigerator.

I was determined to keep myself fully occupied while Liam was away, so that my fears, however totally unreasoning and unreasonable, would be kept dimly in the background. Liam, I explained to myself firmly, was not running out on

147

me. If he was, he'd have taken his car. And he would never do that to me, anyway. Never. Regardless of the fears I'd talked of to Julie last night, I knew for sure his options – the only ones he would ever consider – were simply the police force or returning to farming, and either one of those included me as his wife.

I *knew* that. But human fears are not always reasonable.

So I filled my day with activities. This was the day the Norrises wouldn't be at home for me to take the picture out to show them the completed work, so I decided I would go to the spot Liam had shown me, where we had picnicked beside the river. I would do some preliminary sketches there.

First I called on Sally Miller. I had not seen any of them since I'd had Brent as an overnight guest. Sally seemed genuinely glad to see me and we talked together easily, liking each other. She was an intelligent woman with a wide range of interests and I felt we were developing the kind of friendship which lasts a lifetime, and I was glad. I asked her if they might all come to the cottage and have dinner with me that evening, and my invitation was only partly due to my desire to not have time to wonder why Liam had suddenly gone to Melbourne without any explanation.

'I'd be delighted,' Sally said. 'I'll have to check with Roger, but if you wait a moment I'll phone him.'

Roger, to my surprise and to Sally's obvious relief, agreed.

'What about Rosemary and Brent?' I asked. 'I mean, teenagers often have things to go to, like squash and dancing or something.'

'I don't know of anything they're doing tonight. I'm sure they'd like to come.' Sally smiled. 'Brent and Roger are getting on much better,' she added in the only reference either of us made to the nightmare I had plunged them into.

So I spent some time by the river, sketching from various angles and trying to decide whether I would want to capture the effect of morning light or afternoon light, to get the best of flung shadows and light catching water and tree-trunks. Middle-of-the-day light had a flattening tendency which didn't suit this particular scene, I decided.

Then I went home in time to prepare dinner, and dinner itself went, I felt, remarkably well. We almost seemed like a normal group – if not exactly a family unit, then at least friends. Brent, after initial watchful reserve, relaxed; and Roger, while hardly the life of the party, was pleasant and more inclined to join in general conversation than he had ever been in my presence.

I went to bed feeling I had managed to have a full and productive day, and I even slept quite well.

In the morning I decided I would take the picture out to show Vi and Ivan and wish them and Peter a pleasant holiday, and perhaps try to rouse a little more enthusiasm for the trip in Peter. It was about mid-morning when I drove up to the house. I had lingered around the cottage for a while, wondering if Liam might phone to say when he would be back, but the phone stayed silent.

I was reaching into the back of the car to lift out the now-framed painting, when Ivan came out of the house, a slightly worried frown creasing between his eyes.

'Oh hello, Lyn.' He sounded faintly disappointed. 'I don't suppose by any chance you know anything about Peter?'

'Peter?' I echoed stupidly.

'He seems,' Ivan said as if he couldn't believe it, 'to have disappeared.'

I looked at him for a moment, feeling I hadn't understood what he had said. 'I don't understand,' I said.

'Neither do we. Oh, there's probably some very simple explanation.' He sounded as if he didn't believe that, either. 'We didn't take any notice at first when he didn't show up this morning. He's very independent,' he added. 'Flatly refuses help with getting dressed and all that sort of thing. It might take him ages, but he manages. And breakfast – well, he just comes into the kitchen and gets his own, sometimes very early, sometimes not. Then he goes back to his room, usually, and gets on with his studies.

About an hour ago Vi went to his room to collect a packet of completed assignment papers that were due to be posted to the correspondence school – she was going shopping – and he wasn't there and the papers weren't ready. So she went to find him to finish them.'

He shook his head. 'She couldn't find him. We've looked every place we could think of – called, of course – everything. He's just disappeared.'

There was a mixture of exasperation, alarm and bewilderment in his voice.

Alarm is contagious. It can also cloud reasoning and judgment, so I tried not to let it swarm over me.

I said firmly, 'Peter can't just disappear.'

There are limits to how far you can go in a wheelchair. I didn't say the words, but I knew they were as clear in Ivan's mind as they were in mine.

'Where have you looked? Have you been up to his Fairy Wood? You know he likes to go there and it's one place where the path is good enough for him to take his chair. Or the shed, or Mrs Wishart's flat, or the elm tree in the corner of the garden? I've seen him reading down there.'

'Yes, of course we've looked in all those places,' Ivan said a shade impatiently. 'Vi's gone back to the wood now, but I'm sure he's not there.'

I looked around me: looked down to the valley, my interpretation of which was on canvas in the back of my car. The drop from in front of the house, where the land fell away to give that delightful outlook, was certainly not a cliff, not a sheer drop; but it was a very steep slope, with much low-growing bush and a scattering of trees. If a wheelchair were to get out of control near the edge, it could certainly plunge wildly a short distance before bushes arrested it. Hardly a fatal occurrence, and hardly likely that someone as dexterous with a wheelchair as Peter was would ever get into such a situation, but if he had, such an accident could well injure him.

Ivan saw my look and said, 'I can't imagine he'd ever be in a place where the chair would get away with him.'

Vi came hurrying down the path from the Fairy Wood,

looking tense and anxious. 'Lyn! Do you know anything –?'

'No,' Ivan said.

'I simply don't know where else to look.' Vi looked around distractedly.

'Are you *sure* he's not in Mrs Wishart's place?' I asked. 'He seemed very fond of her and very upset by her death. He might –'

Vi shook her head. 'It was locked, but it was still the first place we looked, and we looked in every corner – every cupboard, even.'

Ivan said, 'Lyn thinks the chair might have somehow got away from him – run down the slope in front of the house and gone over the edge of the escarpment. I guess we have to start wondering about that. We're running out of options. *If* it happened, he could possibly be injured.'

'Are there school holidays at the moment?' I asked.

They shook their heads. 'Why?' Vi asked.

'I just wondered whether possibly Arnold Bright had come over early and taken Peter out somewhere and Peter had forgotten to leave a note to tell you where he'd gone. But obviously that's not the explanation.'

Ivan shook his head. 'Arnold will be at work. Wherever Peter went, he went on his own. So obviously he can't have gone far.'

There was a small silence, and I said, 'Well, let's start looking along the edge.'

We walked – Ivan and Vi in one direction, I in the other, looking for small wheel-tracks, for broken bushes, for any sign that something had plunged down the slope. We called, and paused to listen for an answer.

Nothing.

We met back at the house, having explored that possibility as far as was reasonable, and looked at each other blankly.

Ivan said again, 'He hasn't gone far. He can't have. So where the *devil* is he? Why doesn't he answer when we call?'

'He may have fallen asleep somewhere,' I suggested hopefully.

They both looked as if that remark was stupid beyond

contempt, and they were right, but I was at the clutching-straws stage. 'Let's search the garden and the shed again,' I said, adding quietly, 'and I guess we have to think that he may have met with some kind of accident and possibly be unconscious somewhere.'

We went our separate ways again, Ivan to the Fairy Wood for yet another search, Vi to check the shed and its surroundings, I to explore the garden and close-by areas – all of us, now, soberly searching for an unconscious form flung from an overturning wheelchair to strike his head on stone or post or tree.

It didn't take me long to search the garden and any nearby areas where Peter could conceivably be. Vi, I saw, had gone up to the wood to help Ivan comb through it. I stood irresolutely, simply feeling we were groping through some kind of maze and endlessly coming to a dead-end because we kept following the same paths. There was some unexplored avenue, obviously. Although, glancing down the valley again, I knew the search we had made along the top hadn't been really conclusive. It would be possible for something as small as a wheelchair to plunge down into some of those steep, brush-filled gullies and not leave a readily-discernible path, because there were plenty of tough, springy bushes whose branches would be only momentarily pushed aside and at once would swing back into place, leaving no easy trace of whatever had brushed by. To search the area thoroughly would need quite a number of people actually clambering around the slope through the bush.

For that, help would have to be called in. And at this moment I could see no alternative. Except –

I glanced at the house. I am not prone to enter other people's houses without their knowledge, but it seemed to me that, no matter how unlikely, there was still a possibility Peter was with Arnold Bright. Somewhere. At *school*?

The idea was not entirely absurd. Arnold had felt Peter had been kept away from normal living too much. Perhaps Peter felt that also. If he had asked Arnold to take him to school to let him see if he could cope, he might very well have elected to allow Arnold to believe Ivan and Vi had agreed to it. And, knowing that they wouldn't, had decided to defiantly do it and present them with a *fait accompli*. And be able to point out, effectively, that if he could handle it for one day he could handle it on a permanent basis.

The more I thought of it, the more I believed that was the answer. With a surge of hopefulness, I decided not to wait for Ivan and Vi to come back. I would simply go in and telephone the school.

I asked the young lady in the office who answered the phone: 'May I speak to Mr Arnold Bright, please? It's rather urgent.'

'I'm sorry,' she said pleasantly. 'Mr Bright isn't in today.'

'Isn't in?' I echoed. 'Do you know why? I mean, is he ill?'

'No, he telephoned the day before yesterday to say he had to go to Melbourne on urgent personal business. He said he may be away all week.'

'I see.' The day before yesterday. So much for that theory. 'Thank you,' I said slowly and replaced the phone.

I walked out of the house and across the garden, intending to take the path up to the wood to suggest to Ivan and Vi that it was time to call in extra searchers to cover the steep roughness in front of the house, since a runaway wheelchair plunging down there seemed the only answer. Just before I turned up the hill it occurred to me there was one faintly-possible place I hadn't looked, and I had no idea whether Ivan or Vi had thought of it.

There was a reasonably smooth gravelled vehicle-track down to the little pump shed at the dam, a couple of hundred metres from the house, which was used for water for the garden. It would be a difficult trip in a wheelchair, but not impossible, maybe; and the dam with its clump of reeds at one end was popular with water-birds, I'd noticed. Peter might well have decided to struggle down there with his camera. I hadn't been in the tiny pump-shed, but probably it would make a good hide for photographing wild water-fowl. With a little flicker of anxiety I wondered if it was possible that somehow Peter's chair, in manoeuvering into the shed, might have fouled something in the electric pump-connection.

Most unlikely, I told myself firmly. And most unlikely Peter had ever struggled down that road in his chair. But I would have to make sure, to satisfy myself.

I saw it before I reached the dam, but what it was didn't occur to me. Perhaps my brain simply refused to register it.

By the time I reached the edge of the water I could no longer take refuge in ignorance. An arc of thin rubber tyre, and the spokes of the wheel it was attached to, were showing above the water in the shallows a couple of metres from the embankment of the dam. The rest of the chair was submerged.

Peter. Peter's wheelchair.

I don't know how long I stood there, absolutely stunned. Probably it was only a few seconds. Then, still numbed beyond feeling, I almost mechanically walked around the wall of the dam to the point nearest the chair – nearest, obviously, to the point of entry. I could see the fine tracks of the chair in the dust of the embankment and then in the mud as it had wheeled sharply down the wall of the dam and finally toppled into the water.

I stepped carefully away from the tracks the chair had made, some part of my intellect still functioning enough to tell me those tracks should be left clear for all to see what had happened. And as I looked around, calculating angles and distances, wanting to see how this unthinkable accident could have happened, that still-functioning corner of my brain which seemed to be totally detached from the rest of me saw something even more unthinkable.

Peter had deliberately run his chair into the dam.

There was no other explanation. He would have had a real struggle to get it to the point where it had gone into the water. There was no conceivable reason for doing it except one: Peter had wanted to die.

I sat down on the ground because my legs would no longer support me.

There was no question of foul play, because if anyone had wheeled the chair there their footprints would have shown as clearly as the wheel-tracks of the chair, and there were no accompanying footprints. I supposed it would have been quite possible to stand on solid ground and physically throw an empty chair into the water, but this one had wheeled down, leaving its tracks, and a Peter who had not wanted to die would never have simply sat in the chair and allowed it to run straight into the dam. He could have easily diverted it or deliberately capsized it.

Suddenly I found I was shaking. Not crying. I could cry later. I whispered his name over and over, staring at the gently wind-rippled sheet of water where a pair of black ducks swam unperturbed, and beneath which, somewhere, Peter lay. I think I prayed.

Presently I stood up. There were things to be done. I had to tell Ivan and Vi. I started to walk toward the wood – Peter's Fairy Wood, where his beloved fairy wrens would flicker enchantingly, raising their families each spring, unknowing that anything was missing from their wood – when I heard a car start up and saw Vi driving away, while Ivan walked toward me. Vi, going for others to help search, or to a friend's place perhaps to see if by any chance they had come and taken Peter for an outing.

And I had to tell them to get the police with divers or grappling hooks.

'We wondered,' Ivan said as he came closer, 'whether just possibly Arnold *had* taken Peter out – and the place Peter would want to go would be Mt Bartholomew. He's really keen on that place. And if Arnold took him out – it could have been early, to watch the sunrise or something – and the car broke down, they'd be really stranded there. Vi's gone to check it out.'

'Ivan –' I began.

'It's a long shot, I suppose, but it's really not as unlikely as it might seem, and actually it's the most logical explanation left, because –'

'Ivan,' I said again, and this time something in my face or voice registered and he looked at me sharply.

'What is it?' he demanded. 'Lyn –'

'I know where Peter is,' I said dully.

'What?' He caught me by the shoulders. 'What are you saying?'

'Ivan, I'm sorry. Peter's dead.'

His hands dropped from my shoulders and hung limply by his sides as if there was no longer any connection between them and his brain. I saw some unguessable thoughts wash over him and then he was very still for a moment, blank-faced.

'Dead,' he echoed.

We must have stood simply staring at each other for quite some seconds. Then he said, 'But – how? Where?'

'The dam,' I said. 'A bit of his chair is showing above the water near the wall.'

Ivan swung around to stare down toward the dam. 'But –' There was bewilderment in his voice. 'He couldn't just – fall in there.'

'No,' I said.

'Are you saying –?' He looked back at me. 'Oh, my God. He killed himself. Peter killed himself. All this time –' He stopped.

I nodded. 'Yes. All this time he's been in so much despair, and no one realized. Thirteen years old and he couldn't face living.'

There was another little silence, and then Ivan said, 'I'll have to get the police. The water's pretty deep there in places. Did you see –?' He left the question considerately incomplete.

I shook my head. 'No. The water's not – very clear.'

'No. The police will find him. They're good at finding things in water. I'll phone them now.'

We walked together toward the house, automatically hurrying although haste was pointless. 'Vi,' I said. 'She has to be told.'

Vi, gone to Mt Bartholomew in search of a living boy, thinking of nothing more disastrous than a car which had had a mechanical breakdown.

'Yes,' Ivan said. 'She took my car, which has a car-phone. I'll call her as soon as I've called the police.'

'No, don't,' I said. 'I'll drive out there and tell her. I

think that would be a lot better than hearing it on a phone, or waiting till she comes back. She'll be pretty shocked.'

I didn't add that I desperately needed something to do, something to occupy my mind, anything so that I could put off wondering whether there was something I could have done to help Peter in the weeks I'd known him.

'That's very kind of you,' Ivan said.

I got into my car and drove to Mt Bartholomew, trying very hard to think only of my driving, watching for Vi's car returning from a fruitless trip, though I reflected that she had really been gone only a few minutes before I left to follow her, and I was probably driving faster, because driving fast forced me to concentrate.

Vi had parked at the edge of the clearing, perhaps fifty metres from the shed which was all that remained of the Bartholomews' farm buildings, and I stopped beside her car and looked around.

At first I didn't quite see why she hadn't simply turned around and gone back when Arnold's car wasn't there, but then I realized she would think the car could easily have been parked behind the shed, or simply pulled out of sight behind bushes to provide a photographer's 'hide' for Peter.

I got out and began to walk toward the shed, intending to call Vi's name, when I heard her voice. She was in the shed, and her voice was sharp and distressed.

'What are you doing here?' she was demanding. 'What's going *on*? *Tell* me!'

Instantly all the memory of Vi's fears for her life in that panic-stricken note rushed back. Vi was in trouble.

Without stopping to think that if Vi was in danger what I was doing might well be worse than futile, I ran around to the door of the shed. The door was standing open, but what I saw stopped me as abruptly as if it had been closed and I had run headlong into it.

Vi was standing with her back to the door, and sitting on a wooden packing-case against the wall was Peter.

Eleven

He was white-faced, except for a red weal down one side of his face as if he had come into violent contact with something hard, and there was pure fear in his dark eyes. But he was very much alive.

'Peter!' I cried joyfully. 'Oh, Peter, you're –'

The words died on my lips as Vi swung around to face me, fury in every line of her. And I found myself looking into the dull black muzzle of an automatic pistol.

She was probably as shocked to see me as I was to see the pistol and to understand its meaning, but she had all the advantages. We just stared at each other for several seconds, all still as figures in a tableau.

'Well, well,' Vi said. 'Come in, join the party. Just stand quietly against the wall. And perhaps *you* can tell me what's going on. Did you bring Peter here?'

I was still too stunned to begin thinking. It was as if my entire world had shrunk down to the muzzle of a gun. Death was here, in this shed. A precisely-machined piece of metal in the hand of a woman I had been trying to help. Neither Peter nor I was going to be allowed to leave here alive and we both knew it, though I, for one, had no idea why.

'Answer me!' Vi snapped. 'Did you bring Peter here?'

I managed to raise my eyes from the automatic to her face, and I saw that my first thought – that she was insane – was wrong. She was totally in charge of herself and the situation. The initial shock of my intrusion on the scene was now put aside with a swift new set of calculations in a brain that was not deranged; simply ruthless.

The questions were beginning to rush over me now, as my own brain began to function again. *Why* was Vi doing this? Who *had* brought Peter here, and why? What was going on that I had blithely never suspected?

'Well?' There was a dangerous edge of impatience in Vi's voice. 'Don't stand there like a stunned mullet. Answer me!'

'Mullet,' I said, 'don't stand.'

Since it is patently crazy to provoke someone who is aiming a gun at you, I shall never know why I said it. For a moment I thought she was going to pull the trigger, and I am certain the only reason she didn't was because it might cause complications. Besides, there were factors not known to her and that she needed to know. I didn't have the answers, but she didn't know that, either. And for some perverse, absurd reason, with that senseless piece of insolence, I regained a whisker of composure.

Beyond her shoulder I saw a tiny gleam light Peter's eyes as he realized that however useless I was, at least he had an ally.

'Most amusing,' Vi said after a moment, controlling her anger. 'Now answer me or I promise our little friend here will have more than one bruise on his face. A few more won't matter by the time they pick you both up at the bottom of the cliff.'

My eyes flicked in understanding to the ugly redness on Peter's cheek, already swelling and darkening. 'You hit him with the gun,' I said with revulsion. 'You cowardly slime!'

'Just answer my question. Did you bring him here?'

I had no idea what the best answer would be, but I decided to opt for the truth.

'No.'

'Who did?'

'I've no idea.'

'I told you,' Peter said, and his voice was incredibly steady. 'Arnold brought me.'

Vi was still watching me, since the immobile Peter represented no threat, and I fought not to let the least flicker of surprise show in my face. Whatever Peter was doing here, he didn't want Vi to suspect, and I must not do anything to betray the fact that I knew Arnold had not brought him here, because Arnold was away in Melbourne.

'Really,' Vi said, addressing Peter but still watching me. 'And where is your wheelchair, then?'

'That's why Arnold went away,' Peter said. 'As I was wheeling away from the car one wheel dropped into a hole and it broke some of the bracing underneath, so he took it away to get it fixed. He'll be back any time.'

There was just a shade of uncertainty, even anxiety, in Vi's face. Bravo and bravo, Peter, I thought; you're even sharper-minded than I realized.

'Oh?' Vi said. 'And why did he leave you here?'

'To take the photographs I wanted to try to get.'

'Then where's your camera?'

'I didn't realize I'd left it in the car.'

Oh, Peter, I thought in mixed admiration and anguish: you could have stood your ground in front of a whole pride of charging lions and just gone on taking photographs; and I bet they'd have turned away and left you alone.

Vi Norris, though, was not about to back off. 'How strange,' she said. 'Because I saw it in your room when I was looking for you a couple of hours ago.'

Peter wasn't going to turn and run, either. 'Oh, it wasn't my camera I was going to use,' he said without the slightest hesitation. 'Arnold was going to let me try his new video camera – it's got eight-power zoom and everything.'

'You're lying,' Vi said venomously. To me she added, 'I'm still waiting to hear your version of this fairy-story. Why did you come out here? I thought you had this theory that Peter's chair had got out of control and gone crashing down the mountain in front of the house and was hidden in the undergrowth. You'd like to have had us searching there for hours, I presume?'

With a great effort of will-power I kept my eyes fixed on her face. It required a great effort because, in a morning of shocks, I had just received another.

While he and Vi had been exchanging question-and-answer like duellists thrusting for an opening and parrying attacks, he had quietly been slipping off his thigh-length parka – a move which had slightly puzzled me but not made much impression as being something actually purposeful.

Now, while she was speaking, he looked at me beseechingly, silently begging me to understand, and, putting a finger to his lips, stood up. Without the slightest difficulty.

And, to make sure I understood, silently lifted first one leg and then the other, swinging each easily from hip and knee.

Peter was not in the least paralysed.

How I managed not to look at him or somehow give the whole thing away I am not sure. But I began, very slightly, to understand: understand why he had persisted with deception. Because, God help us both, he had long expected to need this element of total surprise. He had needed his guardians to think he was helpless.

That was as far as my thinking could go in the few seconds I had. That was as far as it needed to go right now. Right now the only thing for either Peter or me to think of was survival. And I thought I understood what Peter had in mind to do.

'Ivan told me you'd come out here because you thought Arnold might have brought Peter here to photograph the sunrise or something, and his car had broken down. I was anxious and just wanted to see for myself if that was right. I couldn't do anything more back at the house.'

Slowly, infinitely carefully, Peter moved toward Vi, holding the heavy padded coat in front of him like a matador's cape, and she still stood with her back to him.

'And,' I added, 'since obviously neither Peter nor I have much chance of leaving here alive, you might at least settle one thing in my mind: did you kill Edith Wishart?'

Vi looked momentarily taken aback. 'Well, well. Smart thinker, are you? Dear Aunt Edith. Of course we killed her. It was so easy it was a joke. Drunken old biddy, but just too nosy. I don't know what made her suspicious, but she was finding out too much about our little Peter.'

I blinked. 'What about Peter?'

'Oh, Peter would come into rather a lot of money if he lived to be eighteen. Since he won't, it comes to Ivan and me as his legal guardians. His grandfather left it that way, silly old fool. Now, as we're wasting time and it may be precious –'

Peter was holding the coat ready, but the gun was still pointed squarely at me, and he knew it. He waited.

I turned my gaze to the floor in the corner of the shed and called on my feeble theatrical abilities, as far as I could remember them from amateur efforts during high school speech-and-drama lessons.

The necessary expression of horror was undoubtedly already on my face, but I let my jaw sag and my mouth open slightly and from years off, heard my teacher's voice telling me not to stare fixedly but to move my eyes as if watching a living, moving object. In this case, I desperately wanted to create the impression of watching something reptilian, large, and definitely venomous. Never mind that the day was cold and any sensible snake would be hibernating – hopefully Vi would react to instinct and not reasoning.

Staring at the corner as if at an emerging object, I whispered, 'Oh, my God.'

There was no reason for Vi to suspect a trap. I was several paces away and no matter how fast I moved I couldn't reach her before she brought the gun to bear on me again. And Peter, as far as she knew, couldn't move off that wooden crate.

She turned her head to look, swinging the gun around toward the corner, away from me.

No reptile could have struck with much more speed than Peter. He flung the jacket blindingly over her head and wrapped it once around, at the same time bringing up one foot to slam into the back of her knee, buckling her legs from under her.

The crack of the pistol-shot as her finger automatically convulsed on the trigger came simultaneously with Peter's shout.

'Run!'

Blinded as Vi was, the bullet splintered harmlessly into the wall. I dearly wanted to grab that gun, but I knew that even though Vi would need a couple of seconds to get free of the folds of the jacket she still had hold of the pistol, and trying to wrest it from her had a ninety-nine per cent chance of being fatal. I obeyed Peter's shout and we both went out of the door at a pace that would have done credit to any rabbit.

It is amazing how fast the brain can function when desperate emergency sends adrenalin charging through the system. Although I had seen it only once before, I remembered the shed door opened outward. Peter and I worked together without a word, each somehow knowing exactly what the other had in mind. I swung the door shut and he dropped into place the heavy wooden bar which fastened the door from the outside.

'The car!' I panted. 'This way!'

'No!' Peter grabbed my arm. 'She can cover the cars from the window with that gun. We'd never make it.'

I saw at a glance that he was right.

'This way!' he said, running. I had no time to think that this was the boy I had only seen sitting apparently helpless in a wheelchair. I ran with him.

'Can she get out through the window?' I asked.

'Yes. It'll be hard – take a couple of minutes. But she can get out.'

'A couple of minutes! We can't get far in a couple of minutes.'

'Far enough.'

It was then I realized where he was going: straight for the cliff edge. '*Peter!* We can't! We've no ropes – and anyway –'

'Don't need ropes. There's a place we can climb down.'

We were at the edge and I looked at the sickening drop and felt the old blind terror of heights that brought painful tingling to my hands and feet.

'I can't, Peter. I'm – no good – at heights. You go. I'll hide somewhere.'

'You can't! The bush isn't thick enough and you can't get

far enough. Lyn, she'll kill you. Come *on!* It's safe. You won't fall. Follow me and don't look down any further than your feet.'

I knew he was right about my survival chances up on the top of the plateau. Vi's opportunity to dispose of us both in an inexplicable 'fall' from the cliff had met with a severe setback, but we still constituted a greater danger alive than dead. I would have been willing to bet that the pistol she had wasn't registered on any police file and if she disposed of it she could possibly put up a convincing front to have our deaths from bullet-wounds blamed on some unknown maniac.

In any case, I was certain, she would be in a murderous rage. Her plans – and Ivan's – had been blown apart. I still hadn't had time to think about those plans and I wasn't consciously thinking of any of those things now. All I had time for was the realization that Peter had a plan for survival and I had none.

I followed him over the edge.

The climb down was not really difficult. I guess it wasn't particularly dangerous, even for a raw non-climber. But I still feel sick when I remember it, and the palms of my hands sweat. Because not for a second could I forget the great depth of air below me, where, farther down, the mountain did fall away in sheer cliffs.

Peter scrambled down quickly and confidently, encouraging and directing me with an occasional quick, 'There's an easier bit to your left. That's it. Great. You're fine. You couldn't fall if you tried.'

It was probably not more than three minutes before Peter said, 'Now we go over this boulder and we're there.'

A great hump of rock was beside us and he scrambled over its shoulder, along the face of the cliff instead of downwards, and as I followed him, trying not to think of what lay below the boulder, I heard the pistol-shot and felt the blow at the same moment, as though someone had punched me on the arm just below the shoulder.

Then I dropped down to stand beside Peter at a gaping hole about a metre and a half wide in the side of the mountain, and we plunged into the shelter of the cave.

But how much shelter was it?

'Peter,' I said, the feeling coming back into my arm with a fierce burning sensation, 'she'll follow us. Is there anywhere in here we can hide? And it's pitch dark in there, isn't it?'

He pulled a small torch from the pocket of his jeans. 'I've got this. I brought two, and the other was in my jacket-pocket, worse luck. She might have found it. But I know something about this cave she doesn't. I found it one day when I was here before. I was going to tell them about it the day I fell. Come on.'

As we spoke he was heading off into the cave with me at his heels. The only caves I'd ever been in were the Jenolan caverns west of the Blue Mountains of New South Wales, and this was a far cry from the carefully-constructed walking paths and steps and hand-rails at Jenolan, all flood-lit to show the way and highlight the beauty of the limestone formations. Here, the floor of the cave was a mass of boulders of varying sizes; the roof varied sharply in height, so that one moment we were walking – if our clambering and stumbling progress could be called walking – in a high-ceilinged chamber, and the next bent nearly double to avoid hitting our heads. I have never been able to understand the fascination caving has for some people, and this was doing nothing to increase my enthusiasm.

The only virtue was that not only would our pursuer find the going as slow as we did, her chances of getting a shot at us were slim. Until we were cornered against a blank wall with nowhere else to go. That, as far as I could see, was the most probable outcome. Peter said he knew something about the cave that Vi didn't. But what? And could he be sure she didn't know? I recalled Arnold had said something about the possibility of this cave and the one on the south face of the mountain being linked, and I wondered if Peter had found that link.

Peter was trying to share the light of his torch with me as much as he could, but just as we entered a larger cavern I failed to see just one more out-jutting piece of rock in the wall, and bumped my injured shoulder on it.

The blaze of pain made me cry out involuntarily, and Peter swung around and turned the torchlight on me. I knew my arm wasn't broken, and the fear of Vi following at our heels had acted as some kind of analgesic, but now for the moment I felt dizzy with the pain.

'Peter, I'll have to – stop a moment.'

I sat down on a boulder. 'You're hurt!' Peter said, coming to me quickly. Blood was still trickling down my arm inside my sweater, saturating the sleeve and dripping off my fingers. 'She shot you!' Fury was in his voice. 'Lyn –'

'I'm all right,' I tried to reassure him. 'It's only a flesh wound. I bumped it just now, that's all.'

'We should bind it with something to stop the bleeding. Can you get your sweater off?'

I shook my head. 'I think I might faint if I tried pulling it off. It's all right. Peter, go on without me. You'll go much faster. I'll hide behind a rock. She'd just go past.'

I knew, in fact, that the boulders which littered the cave floor were not really big enough to hide behind. Peter knew it too.

'No!' he said sharply. 'Besides, it'll take two people to get out, farther along. We'll wait till you feel better. We've got to be at least three minutes ahead of her.'

It was only in retrospect that I realized neither of us, in that desperate flight, ever once referred to our pursuer by name. It was almost as if she had forfeited the right to have a personal identity.

'Peter,' I said as I sat waiting for the world to stop spinning around me, so that I could walk on, 'how long have you been able to walk?'

'Almost always. But I guessed from the beginning – I wasn't *certain*, but I guessed – they meant to kill me, so I thought I'd have a better chance if they thought I was stuck in a wheelchair. I had an awful lot of trouble with doctors because they kept saying they didn't understand it and wanting to do more tests. In the end, because I knew they'd find out and tell on me, I persuaded everyone I was so sick of doctors and hospitals and tests, and they just let me alone.'

'How did you know' – I swallowed – 'they meant to kill you?'

Thirteen. A child still – or he should have been. He wasn't a child, though. The last years of his childhood had been snatched from him by the knowledge that his guardians planned his murder.

'The day I fell, when she and Arnold were going caving on the south face. She sprained her ankle deliberately. I was standing near the car with my back turned and Arnold was getting the gear ready, but I could see her in the wing-mirror of the car. She put her foot between two rocks and leaned over sideways. I didn't understand. It must have hurt like anything. I thought she must have been scared of the south face and didn't want Arnold to know. Then the rope broke while I was abseiling, and afterwards everyone said an old battery had tipped over and spilt acid on it and no one noticed.'

He had turned the torch off to save the batteries, so we were sitting in pitch darkness and I couldn't see his face, but the terse, matter-of-fact way he told the story was somehow horribly chilling, in that it made me realize he had lived for almost a year in the knowledge he was the target for murder, and outwitting his assassins had become a day-to-day way of life.

'She said, afterwards, she hadn't checked the rope,' he went on. 'She was lying. She'd checked it just before we left – I noticed how carefully she looked at it, and when she'd finished Ivan was watching and he said, "Neat, isn't it?" I remembered, because Ivan was never interested in caving and I thought it a bit funny. Then when the rope broke and I fell, I reckoned I understood. So I pretended to be crippled so that I could sneak around and listen when they thought I couldn't be anywhere near. I guessed I'd eventually hear if they were planning to kill me. I wasn't quite sure, till one day I did hear.

'I never understood why, till today – just a while ago, when she told you about my grandfather's money. But I always knew they didn't like me much.'

He flicked the torch on again, its light seeming brighter after the absolute blackness.

'Can you walk now?' he asked anxiously, acutely aware, as I was, of peril closing in behind us.

I nodded. 'Let's go.'

He swung the little beam of light around the cavern, which was not as large as I'd first thought. The cave continued on into the darkness to the left, but he went quickly across to the right where there was a jumble of stone rubble like an ancient rock-fall, and at the top of it a slit in the rock about forty centimetres high and less than a metre wide.

'We go through here,' he said softly, keeping his voice down deliberately so that his words didn't carry. 'Lie flat and worm your way.'

'We can't get through there!'

'We have to. It's all right – we can. It's only like this for a few metres. You're little – you'll get through easily. It might hurt your arm – I'm sorry. But she doesn't know about this. She'll go the other way, and it ends in a blank wall.'

Already he was flat on his stomach, torch held in front of him, sliding by pulling with his hands and pushing with his feet, disappearing like a snake into its hole. I had no choice but to follow.

A few metres, he said. Probably that's all it was. Twenty, thirty, maybe fifty – I have no intention of ever going back to find out. It felt like a thousand. Squirming through something that size that was smooth like a drainpipe would be bad enough. But this was not smooth. The bottom of it – the floor – was dusty and gravelly, and protruding rocks in walls and roof were absolutely perfect for bumping against. I understood very clearly why speleologists wore safety helmets: my head was a succession of minor bruises. We had to drag ourselves through with our arms outstretched in front of us like swimmers doing some kind of severely-restricted breast-stroke, and I mentally thanked God that Vi's bullet had missed the bone in my arm. Had the arm been broken I don't think I could have made it.

As it was, it was bad enough. I had to grit my teeth against the pain, and a couple of times I thought I was going to faint. I think probably shock was beginning to take toll of me. I suppose we were in that tight, twisting fissure in the mountain for not more than ten minutes. It may have been much less. It seemed a very, very long time in which I just forced my body on, lying flat, my face almost on the ground, every part of me bumped and scraped by rock protruberances, forcing myself on almost mindlessly, in nearly total darkness because Peter's body, ahead of me, was blocking almost all the light from his torch. In fact, I'm not sure that he used it all the time. I think, in an effort to conserve the precious battery-life, he crawled some of the time in darkness, too. As I struggled after him I was constantly aware that he was having no better time than I was, except he didn't have a bullet-hole in his arm, though he did have a vicious bruise on his face.

And constantly he murmured encouragement to me. Perhaps to himself also. 'It's not far now. It gets a bit better here; be careful – just where I am there's a low bit, you might bump your head. Don't be frightened, you can't get stuck.'

You can't get stuck.

Mercifully my unreasoning terror of heights doesn't extend to enclosed spaces. No one suffering claustrophobia could have gone through that rock-slit, I'm sure. But though pain and shock, and the thought of an armed killer following, all combined to dull my conscious assessment of the situation, I was unceasingly aware of two thoughts.

The first had been that one of us might actually get jammed in that tunnel and be unable to go either forward or back. Peter said it couldn't happen. I had to believe him. The second thought – though it was hardly real thought, more simply a horrible awareness – was of the incalculable tonnes of rock a few centimetres above us, poised – how securely?

Then suddenly I could see the light from the torch, and I realized Peter was no longer lying in front of me. We were at the end of the tunnel and he was already on his feet and helping me out.

Mind you, the part of the cave we were in was no great shakes, either – just more of what we'd had before: boulders and jutting rock and bend over double and mind your head. But by comparison it was the Great Hall of Parliament House. I was shaking violently, I realized, and panting for breath as though I'd just run a half-marathon.

Peter flashed me a grin of triumph. 'We've made it, Lyn. Sit down a moment. I'll just stack some rocks against the opening. I'm sure she won't find the way, but if she does it'll slow her down.'

I sank down on a stone outcrop, thankful to accept his advice, not quite daring to believe his confidence in our safety. After all, there was a limit to how long we could stay here, even without Vi to deal with. Eventually, even if we waited a day or longer, we had to go back. And only Vi knew we were somewhere in the cave.

Better not, I decided, to let my thoughts run in that direction. I watched my courageous young companion valiantly roll and carry rocks to pile against the tunnel-opening.

'Peter, how did you get here – to Mt Bartholomew? Did you walk?'

He nodded. 'I cut across country last night. I ran my wheelchair into the dam. I thought they'd see it and think I'd drowned, even if the police couldn't find the body. I thought it would give me plenty of time. It was pretty dark last night – there wasn't a moon – and I got a bit lost on the way and it took me a lot longer to get here than I'd thought. It was nearly daylight and I was awfully tired, so I pulled two wooden boxes together and lay on them and went to sleep. I thought I'd be safe. But I slept much longer than I meant to, and she came.'

He paused and looked at me. 'Why did *you* come?'

'I found the wheelchair after she left to come out here in case you'd made arrangements with Arnold to bring you here to photograph something. I came to break the news that you were dead. If only I'd known long ago you needed help –'

Suddenly I stopped as realization hit me. The note. The note to Lillian. *Peter* had sent that note. Had signed Vi's name because who was going to take a thirteen-year-old seriously? The tree across the road, that day that Lillian was to arrive: Peter must have put it there and been waiting on the embankment to jump down and pour out his terrors to the only person he could trust.

And she was on the other side of the world and along had come a total stranger.

'I didn't know about you,' Peter was saying. 'I thought you were a friend of theirs. I didn't know *who* knew what they were doing, or if anyone at all knew. Didn't even know about Arnold, because he was there the day I fell. I *thought* he was all right, because otherwise he'd have made sure of it by letting me abseil on the south face. I didn't know about Aunt Edith, either. There wasn't anyone. All I could do was run away.'

'Where were you going?' I asked weakly.

He shrugged. 'Anywhere. Pretend I was older and try to get work a long way from here. Something like that. Go to a city if I had to – join the street kids you hear about.'

He heaved another rock into place.

'I've known for sure for weeks that they meant to kill me, and how they meant to do it. I heard them planning they were going to take a trip to the Barrier Reef and the islands up there, and they'd take me boating for a treat and one day I'd be drowned and it would all look like an accident. So I knew as soon as they had a date set for this great holiday I'd have to cut and run. But it all went wrong because they didn't see the wheelchair in the dam.'

'You trusted Lillian Ballard.'

He nodded. 'Lillian's great.' Then, 'How do you know I trusted Lillian?'

'I got your note.'

His eyes widened. '*You* got my note?'

'Yes. I thought Vi sent it, of course. I thought *she* was the one in danger. I just did everything the note said, because Lillian wasn't there and I felt I had to do something, even though I'd never seen Vi in my life. So I tried to become a friend of hers, and waited for her to tell me why she was afraid. I didn't understand, but I waited.'

'But – how did you get the note?'

'Peter, I rented Lillian Ballard's cottage.'

Comprehension struck him. 'That's why you came, that day. I was waiting to stop Lillian before she got to the house, to tell her. But of course she never came because she'd gone away, and I didn't know. The man I gave the note to would just give it to you, and I hadn't put Lillian's name on the envelope.'

I had a quick memory of Liam, when I had asked him to describe the woman who gave him the note, saying after a moment's hesitation that he hadn't taken any notice. Unsuspecting, amused by the whole thing, he hadn't wanted to risk causing trouble for a kid who, he would assume, was more willing to part with ten dollars than to be caught out for not delivering a note he'd been supposed to deliver, and then apparently, found he had no time left to do so.

'They were going into town that day,' Peter was saying, 'and I asked to go along for the drive. They were always nice to me. I guess they didn't want me to suspect they were up to something. They went into the supermarket together and I hopped out of the car and gave the letter and ten dollars to the first bike-rider I saw. It was too risky to post it, because while I was walking to a post-box and back someone who knew me might see me. And I couldn't phone Lillian, because there are two extensions of the phone in the house and I could never be sure someone wasn't listening, because I know Aunt Edith did sometimes. Vi and Lillian used to be friends but they had an awful argument about me not going to school, and Lillian never came any more.'

He swung the torch beam around. 'There doesn't seem to be any more rocks I could use. How's your arm? Can you go on?'

I stared at him. 'On? Where?'

'Over there – see, where that sloping bit is.' He snapped the torch-light out, and after a few seconds while my eyes adjusted to the loss of the torch-light, I realized the cave was no longer pitch black. Light, daylight, filtered in, and I realized also for the first time that the air here was fresher, lacking the heavy musty odour.

'There's an opening!' I said. 'But – where does it lead?'

'Up,' Peter said. 'It's a vertical shaft – well, not really vertical, more of a very steep slope. I guess a bit of the roof of this cavern fell in a very long time ago. It comes out in bush on top of the mountain, only a few hundred metres from the shed. I found it one day when I did some exploring of my own in the cave while she and Arnold were trying to find if this cave and the one on the south face were linked. I didn't tell them because they'd have been mad with me for poking about on my own. The opening's awfully hard to find from the top.'

'You mean,' I said as we started scrambling over the fallen rock-rubble, 'that we can get out while she's still trying to find us in the cave?'

'Uh-huh.' He nodded. 'There's no other way out. She'll think we're still in there because to get out we'd have to go back past her, and of course she knows we haven't done that.'

My spirits rose singingly. A jagged hole through the arm seemed a minor detail against the thought of life, sunlight, fresh air, and my car waiting to take us back to the police, and survival.

I remembered something Peter had said earlier. 'Is this,' I asked, 'the place you meant when you said it needed two people to get out?'

'Oh, that. No. I lied. You wanted to stop and I had to make you keep trying to go on, and I couldn't tell you too much for fear our voices would carry, and she'd hear. I knew you'd keep going if you thought I needed you to help.'

'Peter Fisher,' I said with a slight catch in my voice, 'I love you.'

He turned to glance back at me with a grin. 'You're not so bad yourself,' he said.

The climb out would have been tough and demanding if I'd been perfectly fit. Hampered by my good-as-useless arm it was not amusing.

A steeply-sloping, narrow fissure – though spacious by comparison with the horizontal one we had just negotiated – it was rough and full of broken rock which sometimes gave way and slid under our feet, giving a heart-stopping but fortunately false impression that we were about to start a rock avalanche.

As we climbed, the torch was unnecessary, though the light was muted and I realized the entrance was shaded by trees. Perspiration, more from nerves than exertion, trickled down my face and, to judge from my companion's appearance, streaked the dust that was caked there.

Then we were out, pushing through some low-growing shrubs that leaned across the opening. Standing in the open, in tree-dappled sunlight with a cold breeze blowing, and solid ground under our feet, and we were alive.

We looked at each other. Peter was covered in dust, his shirt was torn and blood from a small cut on his cheek had run down to his chin beside the bruise where Vi had struck him with the pistol in an effort to beat the truth from him. But there was a light in his eyes I had never seen before. I thought he looked wonderful.

Because I didn't trust myself to say anything serious without dissolving into tears, I said, 'My hat, you're dirty.'

'Look who's talking,' he said cheerfully.

And we flung our arms – or in my case only one – around each other in a bear-hug of jubilation.

'Well, well, what a touching little scene,' Vi Norris said behind me.

Twelve

For a frozen second I honestly thought I was hallucinating. Heaven knows what Peter was thinking.

It was like some hideous nightmare when some stalking awfulness suddenly materializes in a place where it cannot be.

Vi had been following us in the labyrinth of the cave, and now that we had emerged from musty darkness into sunlight she was here, impossibly, waiting for us. I turned to stare at her.

She was standing where she had evidently stepped from behind the concealment of a thickly-foliaged shrub, that cursed automatic calmly levelled at us as we stood together, a look of triumph on her face. All the time we had simply *assumed* she was following us in the cave, but we had never seen or heard her. We had fled from a non-existent pursuer, straight into an ambush. Peter had been mistaken: Vi had known about this exit-shaft and at some point had realized where we were going.

She confirmed that. 'I didn't know you knew about this way out, but I soon saw by your footprints in the dust which way you were going. So I thought I'd just pop back and wait for you. So much nicer than going through the squeezes.'

She laughed, thoroughly pleased with herself.

Dear God, I thought: this was the woman I'd saved from being crushed under a runaway car: the woman for whose safety I had been concerned for all these weeks.

'This time,' she said to Peter, 'you won't take me by surprise, you cunning underhanded little bastard. You

175

knew. You knew all along what we had planned for you
and you pretended you couldn't walk. Clever little sod,
aren't you? Why didn't you tell someone what the nasty
people were up to?'

Peter was silent.

'*Why?* Answer me or I put a bullet through your friend's
other arm.'

'No one would believe me,' Peter said sullenly.

Vi stared, then laughed. 'No, I guess not. Now, walk,
staying close together. In fact, walk hand in hand, nice and
chummy. Over there.' She jerked the gun-barrel toward
the cliff of the south face.

'And if we don't,' I said, 'how will you explain
bullet-holes in us? It won't look much like an accident.'

'Oh, there's enough places around here to hide a couple
of bodies where you'd never be found, I promise. And you
can take your pick of a quick end via the cliff, or I
guarantee a much less pleasant one if I have to shoot you. I
won't do it very – neatly.'

She paused to let the threat sink in. 'Now walk.'

I don't think either Peter or I had the least intention of
obediently jumping off a cliff, whatever she intended. But
it was a couple of hundred metres to the south face
escarpment, and while we couldn't communicate our
intentions to each other, I think we both felt that at least it
gained us a few moments of time, and something, some
diversion, some opportunity, might present itself.

We looked at each other, he took my right hand in his
left and we turned and began slowly, still numb with
disbelief, to walk.

'Just put the gun down, Mrs Norris,' Liam's voice said
quietly and firmly. 'There's nowhere to go.'

She whirled and fired in one action, as Liam shouted,
'Split! Get down! Go!'

Peter's reaction was quicker than mine. Perhaps he had
been thinking some such manoeuvre was our only chance.
And he wasn't hampered by my terrible fear for Liam.
Peter flung himself to his right, rolling as he hit the
ground and then vaulting over the log of a long-fallen tree.

I saw that much on the edge of my vision as I turned to look fearfully for Liam. I saw him run, crouched over, from cover to cover of the trees, working his way closer, as Vi fired again. I had no time to wonder how he had come to be here. I had only time to feel a leaping surge of fear for him that was even stronger than the hope which came with it.

And for probably three full seconds I simply stood there, stupidly, a perfect target if Vi turned to look back towards us.

'Lyn!' Peter shouted. 'Get down! Go right! Run!'

As he shouted, I saw Liam run again, dodging, weaving. I saw his hands were empty: he was unarmed. He was a policeman, but he was on holiday, and he hadn't dreamed he was stepping into this. In the same split second, as Vi fired again, I understood that he was deliberately letting her catch glimpses of him in order to draw her fire from us, and every moment I stood there increased his danger.

I ran, bent double, to my right as Peter had told me to. Less than ten metres away was a rock among some bushes – not much of a rock as impregnable fortresses go, but a lot more bullet-proof than fresh air. It seemed a fearfully long way and at every one of the few blundering steps it took me to reach it I expected to feel the smashing impact of a bullet.

Then I was crouched behind it and, given some degree of cover from the bushes, I peered around it. I couldn't see Liam. Neither could Vi. She still stood, pistol held in front of her in a marksman's two-handed stance, waiting for a target. I knew Liam was not more than eight or ten metres from her. If she saw him now, at that range, she wouldn't miss. I took breath and prayed that both Liam and Peter would understand what I was doing.

'I can't run!' I almost screamed. 'I can't move. Peter, no! Put that down! Don't – she'll kill you!'

Vi would have needed superhuman nerves not to react. She whirled around, gun at the ready, to confront whatever was happening behind her. It took several moments of sweeping scrutiny to realize that nothing was happening at all, and her two intended victims were out of sight. She hesitated, uncertain, irresolute, feeling her grip on the situation loosening.

It was long enough. Liam dashed out from cover and by the time she had turned half-way back to face him, he hit her with his shoulder in a full crashing footballer's tackle and they thudded to the ground together and the pistol flew from Vi's grasp.

I scrambled to my feet, but Peter was much quicker, sprinting forward to scoop up the gun. Liam didn't need our help. By the time I reached them he had hauled Vi to her feet, her right arm twisted none too gently behind her back, and she was white-faced with rage and shattering failure.

Peter handed Liam the automatic and he smiled at the boy and said, 'Thanks, Peter.' He slipped on the safety-catch and put the gun in his pocket and looked at me, concerned alarm in his eyes.

'Lyn! Your arm!'

'It's all right,' I said. 'It's only a flesh-wound. It doesn't matter. It's all right. You're here and we're alive. Liam, you could have been killed!'

'Seems there were a few of us in that category. Sit down somewhere, Lyn. I think you're about thirty seconds off a faint. I can't release my hold on the prisoner. Unfortunately I'm not carrying handcuffs.'

Peter helped me to a log. To my disgust Liam was right, and faintness was threatening to swamp me. I was angry with myself for being so feeble, but I guess it was the relaxation of tension as much as anything, letting all the traumas of the past few hours catch up with me, and as well I had lost a good bit of blood and my arm was throbbing viciously.

Through the surf-like buzzing of near-fainting I heard Liam ask Peter, 'Did Mrs Norris shoot Lyn?'

'Yes,' Peter answered. 'It must be hurting like anything, and she came right through the cave with it, even through the squeezes.'

I heard Vi give a gasp of pain. 'You're breaking my arm!'

'You couldn't guess how I'm tempted,' Liam answered coldly.

'I've got some strong string in my pocket,' Peter volunteered. 'Do you want to tie her hands?'

'Good man,' Liam said.

Over the next ten minutes or so – while Liam first bound Vi's hands behind her back and ordered her to stand where he could see her, and then cut away my sleeve and used some of his shirt as a bandage for my arm – he elicited most of the story from Peter and me, and, as we began to walk back to the shed, Vi walking sullenly in front, he began to explain what he had been doing.

'Apart from the fact that Glen Harlin was a bit uneasy over Mrs Wishart's death, I simply never had a clue there was anything strange going on at the Norrises,' he said. 'Until the other night at Glen and Julie's you showed that photograph of Peter – the boy tragically confined to a wheelchair. And I recognized him as the boy who'd given me that note and ten dollars to deliver it, and that boy hadn't been in any wheelchair and he could run like a hare. He'd looked dead scared, that day – that was why I took pity on him and delivered the note – but I thought he was just going to be in big trouble somewhere because he'd been skylarking around instead of getting the message delivered by a deadline. Then when I knew he was supposed to be a paraplegic I knew something was terribly wrong.

'So I went to Melbourne – because you'd said that was where the Norrises lived before they came here – to enquire into Peter's background. Did you ever meet your grandfather, Peter? Your father's father?'

Peter shook his head. 'No. I remember they took me to a solicitor's office once, and a man there told me my grandfather had died and left me some money and it could be used for things I specially needed. I asked if there was enough to buy me a good camera and they all seemed to think it was funny, but I got my camera and I didn't think any more about the money. Of course, that was – oh, about two years ago. I was only a kid.'

Only a kid. At not yet fourteen, youth was a long time ago.

'Your grandfather was a wealthy man. He was Italian, with very strict ideas, apparently. He disowned your father because he didn't marry your mother, even when you were born. Your grandfather thought that showed a lack of responsibility, and irresponsible people shouldn't have money. So, as your father was his only child, he left his money to you – making the perfectly natural proviso that if you happened to die before you came into control of the money when you turned eighteen, it would go to whoever were your legal guardians at the time.'

He paused a moment. 'Your grandfather never dreamed he might be putting you in danger, I'm sure. He simply wouldn't think people would be so evil.'

Vi had not spoken a word since he had tied her hands, and, I think without realizing we were doing so, we all talked as if she were not there. Again it was as if by her actions she had become a non-person.

Liam had my uninjured arm drawn through his for support, for which I was grateful, because there was no pathway, and we simply had to step over fallen limbs and stones and push through bits of undergrowth, and though my arm felt better for being bandaged, it still hurt considerably.

'I still don't know how you found us,' I said.

'I'd come back on an early-morning flight,' Liam explained, 'and I went straight to the police station to talk to Glen and the others about what I'd learned from Peter's grandfather's friends and solicitors and the Victorian Police, and the call came in to say Peter had drowned in the dam.'

I saw Vi's shoulders stiffen and she swung around. '*What?*' she said, and I remembered she didn't know that Ivan believed Peter was dead and their mission accomplished, even if by an unexpected turn of events.

'Just keep walking, please,' Liam said in a tone devoid of inflection, and after staring at him for a second she obeyed.

'I followed the police cars out to the Norris place,' Liam
went on, 'and I asked where you were and Mr Norris told
me you'd come here to tell Mrs Norris about Peter and he
was a bit concerned because neither of you had come back.
So I came and saw the cars and I got worried and started
searching. Incidentally, Lyn, I used the phone in the
Norris car to call your father and tell him you were missing
and I was concerned about you. I rather think he'll come
out.'

He looked down at me with a little smile. 'I had no idea,
of course, just how much trouble you were in, or I'd have
been calling the chaps away from searching for Peter's
remains. I might add it didn't half give me a jolt when I
saw him alive and walking.'

He grinned cheerfully at Peter, who flashed him a grin
of delight in return. Then instantly Peter's face clouded.
'They killed Aunt Edith,' he said bitterly. 'She admitted it.'

Liam glanced at me and I nodded.

'Did she now? That's helpful. Mrs Wishart must have
suspected something, Peter, because I found she'd had a
private investigator asking the same questions I was asking.
And,' he added, 'so was Arnold Bright. I met and talked
with him. He was in Melbourne, too, making his enquiries.
Apparently eveyone had remarked how Peter had
changed since his accident. Arnold Bright said it suddenly
hit him, the day of Mrs Wishart's funeral, that Peter was
afraid – so afraid he trusted no one. And for the first time
Arnold wondered if Peter knew what no one else
suspected: his fall was meant to happen. Only Mr and Mrs
Norris could have engineered it, and surely the only
motive would be money. So he set out to discover just who
Peter's real family were, and whether Peter had inherited
much from them. Arnold felt that until he knew that, he
had no grounds for his suspicion. So Mr and Mrs Norris
were not quite as safely beyond suspicion as they thought.'

Peter said soberly, 'I'm glad Aunt Edith and Arnold
weren't – in it with them. I wasn't sure. I wasn't sure about
anyone, not even Lyn. Only Lillian, and she'd gone away.'

'Lillian? Oh, yes. The lady who was meant to get the note

I gave to Lyn. You know, ninety-nine times out of a hundred – more – it's best to go to the police with a problem like that. We don't usually blunder in, boots and all, in such situations. But this time – I don't know. I can't honestly say either of you was wrong in deciding to keep us out of it. Hello,' he added as we emerged into the more open ground around the shed, 'we have a visitor. I guess it's your father, Lyn.'

A car was just drawing up, and the driver opened the door to get out. 'Ivan Norris,' I said.

He got out of the car and stood staring at us, shocked past immediate reaction to what he saw. Still a good-looking man, some part of my brain noted; no one looking at him could ever guess the rottenness that lay beyond the attractive façade.

'*Peter!*' he said incredulously. 'What –?'

Perhaps Vi gave him some kind of signal, perhaps he just began to understand from the look on her face that disaster had struck them. His eyes fixed on Liam. 'Who the hell are you?' he demanded.

'Detective Senior Sergeant Liam Stuart, New South Wales police,' Liam answered. 'I have to place you under arrest, Mr Norris, for –'

'Like hell you will!' Ivan snapped.

He flung himself back into the car, turned on the ignition and, foot hard down, spun the car around in a screaming turn. I saw Liam's hand go to Vi's gun in his pocket, then he shook his head.

'He can't go far,' he said.

He was right. A four-wheel-drive pick-up truck with 'Miller's Plumbing and Draining' painted on the side was coming up the narrow track and the driver spun the wheel to swing his vehicle across the roadway, blocking it. As Ivan hit the brakes and screeched to a halt in a cloud of dust and gravel, Roger Miller leapt out of his truck. Ivan's instincts were aimed blindly at escape, and he also was out of his car and running, but my father's agile lean toughness was far too good, and in a few strides he had hold of Ivan by the collar and in a swift, twisting movement flung him to the ground and in another moment had his right arm twisted hard behind his back in the same manner Liam had disarmed Vi.

Roger marched his captive back to where we stood. Ivan looked from one to the other of us and then erupted in a stream of obscenities.

'Shut up,' Vi said wearily and unexpectedly. Equally unexpectedly, he obeyed.

But I was looking at my father, and I shall remember the black fury in his face as long as memory lasts me.

His eyes were on me, but I knew I wasn't the object of his anger. 'You're hurt!' he said. 'What happened to your arm?'

'I'm all right, Roger,' I tried to reassure him.

'Did this crawling piece of filth have anything to do with it?'

'Only indirectly. His wife shot at me.'

'Were they in it together? Whatever it was?'

Fearful of what he might do, I hesitated, bewildered by the intensity of his rage. I was vaguely aware that Liam, in doing nothing to take charge of the situation and Roger's prisoner, seemed to be deliberately holding off to see what Roger would do.

'*Were* they?' Roger demanded.

'Yes. But –'

Even if Liam had wanted to intervene, what happened next was so quick he would have had no opportunity. Roger swung Ivan around to face him and before the bigger man had time to duck, crashed two smashing blows into his face. More caught by surprise than physically stunned, Ivan stumbled to hands and knees, and Roger again hauled him to his feet, right arm twisted up behind his back.

Just as Vi had done in Liam's grip, Ivan gasped, 'You're breaking my arm!'

'Not yet,' Roger said grimly. 'But I'll break it, all right, and a few other assorted parts of you as well, if you don't talk. I've waited nearly twenty years for this. I've stalked you, you walking sewage; I've watched you and I've waited. I knew you'd be up to some kind of rottenness. I didn't know what it was, and I still don't, but I knew it would be something, because you're too greedy ever to be satisfied. I don't know what this is all about, but somehow you've hurt my daughter.'

He wrenched Ivan's arm and brought a yelp of pain from him.

'Stop it!' Ivan moaned. 'Who are you? What do you want? What are you talking about? I don't know you.'

'Twenty years and a beard and another name do make a difference, don't they? Remember another plumber you knew once, briefly?'

Realization hit Ivan Norris and me at the same time. 'Sutton!' Ivan said, and the colour drained from his face.

'Sutton,' Roger agreed. 'And now, in front of witnesses, you will tell what happened that night twenty years ago, at a jewellery store. You will tell, or I will break you up piece by piece.'

He meant it, and Ivan knew it. He looked at Liam, who still stood passively. 'You're a cop,' he pleaded. 'Stop him!'

Liam said calmly, 'I haven't noticed him doing anything untoward. The law permits a civilian to use as much force as is necessary to restrain a miscreant. Besides, I find the conversation fascinating.'

'You –' Whatever unpleasantness he was about to call Liam was cut off by Roger applying more force to Ivan's arm.

'Start talking,' Roger ordered.

'I can't think,' Ivan panted. 'My arm's – hurting too much.'

Roger released his grip entirely and stepped back. 'Sit on the ground,' he ordered.

'Wait a second,' Liam said, and a gleam of hope showed in Ivan's face. It died rapidly as Liam added, 'First, turn around and raise your hands.' He looked at Roger. 'Check him for hardware,' he said. 'The Norris family seem to make a habit of carrying guns.'

'That figures,' Roger grunted, and ran his hands over Ivan. 'Nope,' he said. 'No accessories.'

'Maybe he dressed in a hurry this morning,' Liam said pleasantly. 'Go ahead, he's yours. Just sit on the ground as you were told, Mr Norris.'

Ivan obeyed, holding his right shoulder. 'Now talk,' Roger said. 'From the beginning. Where did we meet?'

'In a pub,' Ivan muttered sullenly. 'You were drunk. You were bragging that because you were a plumber you knew a lot of places you could get into if you wanted. Even that jewellery store that had that big publicity-stunt display of diamonds that were unset stones. I – knew a bit about getting safes open, but I knew there'd be an alarm system. So I started talking to you, and you agreed to do the job with me.'

'Yes, I did,' Roger said bitterly. 'You made it sound so good, so bloody harmless. And I was a young fool, and greedy, like you. We could make as much in one night as I could earn in five years or more. And the stuff would all be insured. We wouldn't even be hurting the jeweller. You needed me to get in through the roof, because I knew that was the way to beat that particular alarm system. I could turn it off and let you in through the door. You couldn't get in through the roof because you're scared stiff of heights. Have I got it right?'

Ivan nodded. 'Yes.'

Good grief I thought: Ivan Norris and I have something in common. That's why he could never go climbing or caving with Vi and Arnold: like me, he suffered acrophobia.

'And,' Roger said, standing with every muscle of his body tense, 'I asked about the security patrolman. You said you knew his routine exactly. "No problem," you said. "There'll be no risk he'll interrupt us. I'll organize the timing." *Didn't you?*'

'Yes.'

'Talk on.'

'You got in. I knew the security patrol's routine. He came around too often to be sure we'd finish the job between rounds. I knew he always checked back doors as well as front doors, so I waited with some sort of wrench from your tool collection. He never saw or heard me till I hit him. You let me in. I knocked off the safe and we cleaned the place out. I was going to play it straight with you, you fool. Half shares in the loot. Clean split.'

He was sitting, crouched, staring at the ground. None of us moved.

'When we came out, you found the watchman and you went off your brain because I'd killed him. You'd never make big-time,' he added, a flicker of scorn rising in him even then. 'You made me take all the loot. Threw away a small fortune. Kept saying you wouldn't touch it.'

'And told you to go to hell,' Roger said.

For the first time Ivan looked up at him. 'I never understood why you didn't tell the world about me.'

'You'd never told me your name, had you? Not your real name. And you'd told me you were booked on a flight to Bangkok or somewhere. You'd be out of the country. And even if you were caught – if anyone believed me enough to look for you – you'd say I'd killed the patrolman. And what difference would it make? I'd been involved in a crime in which a murder was committed. That put that murder on me whether I swung that wrench or not. So, no matter where you went or what you did, I planned to find you when I got out. And kill you.'

Fear flared in Ivan's face, and Vi said, 'Stop him!'

'Oh, don't worry,' Roger said drily. 'I changed my mind a long time ago. Killing you would let you off too lightly. I want you to do the same long ghastly years inside that I did. I've just waited for the excuse to make you talk in front of witnesses who know you for the filth you are.'

He looked at Liam. 'Did he say you're a cop?'

Liam nodded.

Roger ran his fingers through his hair. 'My daughter and a *cop*?'

'There's no accounting for taste,' Liam agreed cheerfully.

'I don't know about Lyn's taste,' Roger said, 'but *you* certainly know how to pick a great girl.'

'He saved my life,' I told Roger. 'Mine and Peter's.'

Roger looked him over and suddenly he smiled and held out his hand to Liam. 'Then I guess he'll do,' he said.

Then he turned and looked at me for a long moment.

'Hey, kid,' he said, and he and I were hugging each other, and for us the nightmare was over.

To my total disgust the doctor who examined my arm said it needed some minor surgical repairs or I would have some impairment in the use of it, and that meant I would have to spend several days in hospital. Peter went to stay with Arnold Bright, and made frequent, exuberant visits to see me. With the resilience of youth, he seemed to be rapidly leaving the awful months behind him. Between him and Liam they kept me abreast of happenings in the outside world, and Roger and Sally, with Rosemary and Brent, came twice to see me, showing every sign of becoming a true family unit, even though there might still be a few difficult moments.

Liam had told me that with the aid of international police co-operation he had located Lillian Ballard and she was coming home to apply to have Peter given into her care. 'With,' Liam added wryly, 'the proviso that should Peter die before coming into control of his inheritance it will all go to charity – Lillian's idea. But don't tell Peter she's coming. She especially asked it be kept a surprise.'

Glen Harlin had been to see me in his official capacity, to get a statement concerning Ivan and Vi. Julie, his wife, dropped in to visit. It seemed a very long time since Liam and I had been to dinner in the Harlin household just a few evenings earlier. Julie asked me whether Liam had decided whether or not to stay in the police force.

'Not really,' I said. 'He has another month's leave. I think he might go on being a policeman for a while. I don't mind, either way.'

'Well,' Julie said, smiling, 'he certainly knows now that he won't go to pieces if he's confronted with a loaded gun.'

I nodded gravely. 'And if he does decide to leave the force, it will be because he wants to, not because he has to. As you pointed out the other night, that's what he so badly needed to know.'

It was on the third afternoon of my stay in hospital that Lillian Ballard arrived. Peter had come in to visit, and so had Sally and Roger. Somehow – probably from the estate agent's comment, all those weeks ago, that Lillian was 'an adventurous soul', I had formed a vague impression of someone twenty-five, tall, angular and with a forceful voice and somewhat overpowering personality, replete with jangling bracelets and outrageously mod clothes.

The woman who appeared in the doorway of my hospital room was possibly fifty, tall, certainly, but impeccably dressed, with greying auburn hair, a quietly charming smile and laughing brown eyes. 'May I come in?' she asked.

'*Lillian!*' Peter cried joyfully, swinging around and catapulting himself into her arms.

I shut my eyes and sank back thankfully into my pillows. I had no further need to worry about Peter.

When the initial excitement had settled down and introductions had been made, Lillian said, 'Of course you must come back to the cottage when you get out of here. You're still renting it, actually, so you can send Peter and me off, if you like. But there's room for three and you'll need someone to look after you a bit.'

'We'd love you to stay with us,' Sally said, 'if that's more convenient.'

'And where,' Liam asked from the doorway, 'do I fit into these plans?'

'May I suggest,' I said, holding out my uninjured hand to him, 'an early wedding might be in order?'

He took my hand tightly. 'Sounds reasonable to me,' he said.